Merry Christmas!

A TWENTY-FIRST-CENTURY REIMAGINED VERSION

OF CHARLES DICKENS'S *A CHRISTMAS CAROL*

GF Newman

Published by
Legend Press
51 Gower Street
London WC1E 6HJ
info@legendtimesgroup.co.uk
www.legendpress.co.uk

in association with
Five Seasons Press
41 Green Street, Hereford HR1 2QH
www.fiveseasonspress.com

PRINT ISBN 9781917163606
EBOOK ISBN 9781917163613

Typeset in 12.5 on 16 Arno
at Five Seasons Press HR12QH UK

Double BAFTA winner GF Newman has written a dozen+ novels, as many television films, plus 27 feature-length tele-plays *Judge John Deed*, which he created and produced.

His debut novel, *Sir, You Bastard*, was a cause célèbre; fol-lowing his television debut, the mini-series, *Law & Order*, Members of Parliament called for his prosecution for sedition; his debut stage-play *Operation: Bad Apple* was another cause célèbre. He wrote and created BBC Radio 4's longest running drama series, 58 plays from his novel, *The Corrupted*, a fic-tional 'history' of the crime-business-politics nexus from the 1950s to the bank crash of 2008. His last previous novel is in the Judge John Deed series, *Guilty – Until Proven Otherwise*; his latest is *Merry Christmas!*

Prologue

A SMALL LIGHT APPEARED OVER the River Thames, heading upstream and getting brighter by the minute. Was it a star of some sort? Too low, he decided, as it skimmed the water, skilfully avoiding the few small craft that were chugging along. Perhaps it was a drone? No, for as it got nearer, he could now see it was Father Christmas riding on a present-laden sleigh pulled by a single reindeer. With him was a medium-sized black and white mongrel dog. Suddenly, the sleigh pitched up and flew through Tower Bridge, then, pitching up higher, it flew over London Bridge as snow began to fall. The sleigh veered off to the right and across the dome of St Paul's Cathedral, then on past the Royal Courts of Justice and finally dropped down to Great Ormond Street Children's Hospital.

The sleigh came to a halt on the open ward with snow falling off it to form small puddles as two dozen or so sick but nonetheless excited children crowded around, open-mouthed in disbelief at this presence and their sudden good fortune. Some started stroking the reindeer while others patted the dog as Father Christmas merrily passed out parcels to the eagerly reaching hands. It wasn't immediately clear who was deriving the greatest pleasure from this, the man in the red coat with the white beard or the children as they ripped open their packages. Each found just the present they longed for, accepting that this magical person knew all along what they most desired.

Now the black and white dog began to bark, causing Father Christmas to turn. On turning in the direction indicated by his four-legged companion, concern at once clouded the old face – which under the whiskers wasn't so old. There at the end of the ward, staring forlornly through a window was a tearful boy of eight years and seven months, shivering like he was always on the wrong side of the window, always looking in and not sharing any of the joy here. Father Christmas froze as if instantly made of ice. Terror crept over his face when he gave a huge sneeze and instantly disappeared.

Chapter 1

A LESS THAN JOLLY Father Christmas with rheumy eyes and a streaming nose from a vicious head cold turned away from the seventy-five-inch television screen on display in the window of PC World and sneezed again, blasting a billion germs everywhere as a little customer at his side tried to claim his attention. The little customer dressed in a hooded anorak with a Star Wars emblem on the front wasn't managing to make any headway with him.

It was Christmas Eve and snow was falling on the adjacent street market, a rare occurrence that was adding to the excitement of last-minute shoppers, who all appeared in a hurry to get the shopping done and move on to their celebrations. Everyone seemed to be pushing and shoving their way through the crowded market where some of the fruit and veg stalls had been seasonally replaced with stalls of tinsel and toys, which people were grabbing in a frenzy.

The less-than-jolly Father Christmas was immune to all the rising hysteria as he stamped his booted feet and slammed his gloved hands together, trying to keep warm on this raw afternoon. There was no source of warmth available to him, even the chestnut seller's brazier was too far away. But for the fact that this Father Christmas had something other than festive celebrations on his mind, he would have been home in bed. Instead, he shivered as he walked his short beat, remembering to occasionally ring his handbell for effect and ignored the collective cacophony around him; continuing also to ignore that young customer who tugged persistently at his coat, still trying to get his attention. With no concern to spread even a little Christmas cheer, he was focusing instead on some ratty-looking premises, the entrance to which was squeezed between a discount shop and one occupied by a large four-chair barbering shop without customers. Through the door he was watching slipped a number of frightened-looking Asian and Middle Eastern women. Father Christmas pulled a bottle of Benylin from his tunic and took a big swig of the cold-crushing liquid before returning it to his pocket as the persistent customer finally poked him hard with a Space Invader gun.

'Get lost, kid,' Father Christmas growled.

Undeterred and having at last got his attention, the Space Invader kid rattled off his awesome Christmas list. 'A Play Station, an iPhone, an Apple watch, pods, Spiderman suit, off-road bike and an electric scooter, Lego, skateboard, and eh . . . what else? What else do I want . . . ?' he said with a sense of panic in case he'd missed anything.

'Rich parents, I should think,' Father Christmas said helping him out. 'Get lost, I won't tell you again.' His whole attitude reflected how he felt in the frigid air with this rotten head cold that brought forth another huge sneeze.

Pushing the Space Invader kid aside, he circled back towards the ratty premises in time to see other downtrodden-looking women emerge – doubtless benefit cheats. These he tried to keep in sight as they began to get lost in the crowded market and soon disappeared altogether. Impatiently ripping off a glove, he plunged his hand into his voluminous tunic, pulling out his smart phone. He hit a number on speed dial, which didn't get a speedy response.

It soon became clear that this was no largesse- or good-cheer-dispensing Father Christmas, other than in his day-dreaming, which was a rare occurrence. Under those stuck-on white whiskers and eyebrows, he was the unhappy-looking, hard-dealing, never-give-an-unlucky-sucker-a-break, Department for Work and Pensions strike force officer, Eddie Scarr. Not only did he have a bad cold and an equally bad attitude, but this thirty-nine-year-old was carrying both a lot of guilt and an equal amount of anger.

'This sweatshop's jumping. Get down here. Now!' he barked when the phone was eventually answered.

'Office suite' was how an estate agent's blurb might have de-scribed this collection of dingy, low-ceilinged, low-rent inter-connecting rooms which looked like they had last been refur-bished in the '60s. They were overcrowded with battered metal filing cabinets and battered metal desks, each with a phone and a computer – their salute to modernity – with a num-ber of moulded plastic chairs, several of which were broken. The motley collection of the Department for Work and Pen-sions strike force investigators who moved between the furni-ture looked themselves like the deceptive claimants they daily tracked down. Some were ferrying booze and plastic glasses to a central desk, others were bringing in takeaway food, while others helped move desks to make space. The music that was pumping out of someone's sound system, heating up the party atmosphere, was making it difficult for overweight, unshaven Mike House to hear what was being said. Having reluctantly picked up the phone, he was in the mood to party and didn't really want to hear, especially not for having identified work-obsessed Eddie Scarr.

'I didn't get that, Eddie . . . What was that? Speak up, can't you?' Without covering the phone, he shouted, 'Keep it down!' more for effect than any desire to hear. Then into the phone again. 'You sound like you're under water, Scarr. You should be in bed with that cold, not worrying about work.'

'Get back here, you dossers,' Scarr was shouting out of the phone. 'We'll capture this whole parcel of dodgers – deliver the sweatshop owner a Christmas present he won't easily forget.'

'Give us a break, Eddie! On Christmas Eve? If we do a raid now, we'll likely be tied up for half the holiday.' Despair was edging into his voice, for he knew what Eddie Scarr was like. All he seemed to care about was making his fellow man's life a misery.

The flint-looking strike force supervisor, Belle Moran, stepped from her office in time to hear this exchange. She was aware that Eddie Scarr was out on the street doing what he was best at; although she would support him, she refused to feel sorry for him. Being fairly plain in her appearance she compensated for this in her stylish manner of dressing, but never overcompensated by overdressing. Apart from seven-year-old Teddy, her daughter whom she doted on and spoiled, Belle, a single mother, lived with a number of disappointments and regrets in her life, only didn't dwell on them. Instead, she concentrated on work and was good at what she did.

'The quicker you do it, Mike,' she said in a firm voice, 'the quicker the party starts. Right.'

'It's already started, boss.'

Belle gave him a 'tough' shrug and, having left some papers on the nearest desk for them to deal with immediately after the holiday, she turned back into her office.

In order to keep sharp as he waited, Scarr now focused his attention on the market stallholders, mentally noting who there was likely a working claimant. He had a nose for such people; even with a head cold he could sniff them out. Without warning, a snowball smacked into the back of his neck, infuriating him as some of it found its way into his clothes, adding to his discomfort and making him shiver more. Turning, he saw the Space Invader kid scooping up another handful. The little bastard! Scarr grabbed up a handful of snow and started after him and hurled it, then scooped up another handful intent on shoving it down his neck. His first snowball missed the Space Invader kid and hit someone else, who, seeing Father Christmas throwing handfuls of snow, must have thought it was a good-natured snowball fight, so threw some at Scarr.

Soon other people joined in with this fun, including an open-faced man in his early 30s who was laden with shopping bags, which he set down. This was Bob Carter and he participated in this with great enthusiasm, appearing not to have a care in the world. Bob Carter had that unique ability to live in the moment right up until he hit the buffers. That was now. For when he looked up, he found himself staring directly at Father Christmas, whose cold dark eyes beneath those frothy white brows were instantly recognisable to him.

In that same instant, Scarr recognized Bob Carter, even

though he was the last person he expected to see there. Both momentarily froze in disbelief. Was this going to be a Christmas truce? Unlikely.

'Bob Carter —' Scarr hissed breathlessly as he recovered his surprise.

The fugitive, which was Bob Carter, glanced around nervously as Scarr tried to rip off his snow-encrusted whiskers and only half succeeded. Carter's immediate escape was momentarily impeded by other snow-ballers, but then a Romanian man wearing a thick hooded parka who was coming out of the premises under surveillance gave him the opportunity. Darting across the pavement, he caught the door then slammed it once inside.

Momentarily forgetting the misery of his cold, Scarr flew after him and burst through the door with sheer brute force, completely snapping the lock.

The roar of electric sewing machines that filled the grim-looking, dust-hung, first-floor workshop was non-stop with a crowd of some thirty or more Middle Eastern and African women bent concentratedly to their work, sewing garments for Peter Jones. Many were clearly modern trafficked slaves, brought into the country for the purpose – they didn't even dare to look up as Bob Carter raced through the long room towards the fire exit shouting 'It's a benefits raid!' with Father Christmas chasing after him. At first no one reacted but slowly the warning caught like a bush fire and chaos broke out around the room. Two men fled after Bob Carter with Scarr close on their heels. Some women, now deserting their machines, unwittingly impeded his progress.

'Out the way! Out the way,' Scarr shouted, doubting if any of them understood the words, but certainly they got the message as he barged through the fire escape door.

Beyond it the iron stairs were slippery with snow and one of the two men following Carter, familiar for being grossly fat, slipped and was blocking the stairs. Without bothering to stop, Scarr leaped over him and past the other man. The renegade Carter was his target.

Slipping and almost falling as he raced out between the rear of the buildings, Scarr burst on to a busy street, but had lost sight of Carter. What he saw instead was a black and white cur of a dog coming across the road towards him with no regard for a bus, going faster than it should have been in these conditions, heading directly for it. In a moment of instinctive madness, Scarr stepped out and grabbed the dog by the scruff, dragging it from the path of the bus and on to the cycle lane. There, for his rescue efforts, he got hit by a pedal taxi. The driver was dressed as an elf and had a hoop of jingling bells attached to the handlebars.

'Get on your sleigh, you bloody idiot,' the elf called out as he manoeuvred his pedal taxi around Scarr, and went on his way, rear lights winking as if in silent mockery at his being such a dolt.

Sitting on the kerbstone recovering, he looked round at the dog who was squatting on the pavement in the snow watching him. He could almost imagine the dog was smiling. Bob Carter was long gone.

'You could have at least bitten that cheeky bloody elf!' Scarr said irritably. 'Another benefits fraudster, no doubt.'

He waited, as if expecting the dog to reply, and sneezed, blasting another billion germs out into the atmosphere, deeply sorry not to have captured Carter. He owed him for betraying his partner. Now that he knew he was around, it was easy to guess where he'd find him.

Two battered white unmarked DWP Transit vans pulled up on the edge of the market, blocking the road. Mike House struggled out of one with a gang of strike force officers, none displaying one bit of enthusiasm for this raid and none of them bothering to greet Scarr as he approached them. He was equally hacked off at them for taking so long to get here.

'What kept you?' he wanted to know.

'Can't you ever stop? It's Christmas, Eddie –' hopefully appealing to some latent spark of merriment in him.

'Best time to catch people,' came the uncharitable reply. 'C'mon.' He led the charge along the crowded pavement, the others following like they had lead weights in their boots.

In the sweatshop the earlier panic had subsided and the women were again back-bent at their sewing machines, overseen by Jan Kraske, the owner of this enterprise – something he would try to deny.

At once Scarr broke the power circuits and plunged the place into silent gloom, then immediately put just the lights back up so that no one could slip away. The women watched in bewildered silence while the sweatshop owner ran forward waving his arms like an agitated semaphore to protest this interruption of his business.

'What? Why? Clothes be ruined. Business be ruined.'

Scarr produced his DWP warrant card and flashed it in front

of Kraske. 'You've got people here working illegally and some claiming benefits. Now we want everyone's name and address. First you. You are?'

'Oh me? Who me, sir?' Kraske said with a suddenly barely decipherable accent. 'Me, I just visit here, sir. Yes, visitor.'

'You've still got a name, brother – the one your family gave you.'

'Oh, yes. You want name, sir.' Scarr sighed, knowing what the game was with this guy. 'Me, sir. Yes, it Peter Jones, sir.'

'That's a start,' Scarr said reasonably. 'And what address do you have, Peter Jones – apart from the address of your famous store on Sloane Square?'

The other strike force officers were standing around smiling, enjoying this exchange. Most of them were happy for Scarr to make the running here, and most other places they raided.

'Yes, sir. My address, it 15 Gloucestershire Terrace, sir. Baizewaiter.'

'You mean Gloucester Terrace, Bayswater,' Scarr said, typing information into his phone. 'Who are all these people, Mr Jones?' He didn't look up from his screen.

'I not know. They come ask borrow machines. Some no speak English.'

'Then how do they ask to use the machines? You speak Amharic, Bengali, Nigerian, Khoe-Kwadi, do you?' he asked, now glancing around the anxious faces of the women waiting at their machines. He turned back to his phone as the answer he was after appeared. 'Peter Jones doesn't live at Gloucester Terrace, Bayswater.' Scarr smiled, knowing they would have a good result here. As he did on almost every raid he made, first having done his homework. There wasn't a single scrounger, neither walking upright nor in a wheelchair, who could get the better of Eddie Scarr, and he was proud of the fact.

Soon they had everyone identified, with the wholly illegal immigrants set to the side. One of these who Scarr passed with barely a glance, was a prematurely old Ethiopian woman tagged as Mrs Achebe. She was now carefully gathering up her meagre possessions along with her three young children. She looked old enough to have been their grandmother for at a mere twenty-eight she had the face of someone thirty years older. He guessed why she had the children here: probably no place else for them to be with any safety. Tears slipped from under Mrs Achebe's tired eyes, but Scarr refused to be affected in any way by them, tears being a familiar ploy. Many times had he witnessed this cunning trick to move him and tug at the heart strings. His heart was sufficiently hardened through long experience and he had no intention of letting it soften as it would be to his cost.

'We go back to Ethiopia, sir?' she asked in broken English. 'We go?'

They would be going somewhere, but Scarr doubted it would be back to her country of origin, rather to some over-priced hotel as guests of the State, with the poor, overburdened taxpayer footing the bill. The situation made him angry. They might have had good cause to escape their own country, but here wasn't the solution. Anyway, these, like the other ille-gals, weren't his concern; they would be passed on for another Government department to deal with. He simply moved away without answering her and pursued Mike House, who was not only the largest and most untidily dressed member of the team, he was certainly the laziest. He had done nothing but complain about how they would all be missing Christmas at this rate.

'You could round them up a bit faster, then we'd get done sooner,' Scarr told him evenly, but felt like kicking him up the backside.

'What's it to us if she and the others stay or get sent off somewhere? Makes no bloody difference,' he whined. 'Look, if chummy pays his dues, we're out of here.'

This was going to be done right as far as Scarr was concerned, he didn't care how long it took. He ignored this man's appeal to his partner, Taff Thomas, who wasn't in fact Welsh, but was called Taff because of his family name. The faux Welshman loved to party like Mike House. Unlike him however, he wasn't a whiner, but an easy-going, friends-with-everyone wheedler. Only Scarr wouldn't be wheedled.

'Eddie,' he said expansively, 'we don't wanna be working over the holiday. Look, you're already dressed for the party – we got a nice surprise for you back at the office. C'mon.'

Glancing around the room, Scarr was met with a mixture of worried and expectant faces – mostly from the strike force. Most of them were only good for partying in his opinion; none of them pulled their weight, and he didn't like surprises anyway.

'What do you say, Eddie, boy? Ready for a good time?'

'Call Immigration,' Scarr said in a flat tone. 'Let's get started.' He nodded Jan Kraske, the 'fessed-up sweatshop owner, towards the office, knowing Taff Thomas would be rolling his eyes or shaking his head at his colleague.

'Someone ought to take him out, just once, and show him a good time,' Mike House said, clearly not caring that Scarr heard. 'Oh yes, someone did once – took him to a funeral!'

Chapter 2

TREADING CAREFULLY ON THE snow, trying not to slip over with his bags, Bob Carter crept warily along the street in the shadows, passing the house he was watching from the opposite side of the road. Spooked by his near-miss with Eddie Scarr earlier that evening had made him extra cautious now. It was Christmas and he had foolishly let his guard down. As far as he could tell there was no one on the street ready to collar him; no suspicious-looking vehicles parked with the engine running to keep the watchers inside warm. Noise erupting from a house further along the street as a door suddenly opened made him tense, ready to run, but it was only a neighbour putting out some rubbish. He stepped between two parked vans, eyes darting left and right – not to make his crossing safe but to make sure he was safe.

The semi-detached house where his family was appeared quiet, a small Christmas tree lighting up the window. Was it safe? He decided it was, but then a car appeared, crawling towards him, lighting him up. Bob darted across the road out of its way. The car with two women in it continued on without stopping, so he approached the house and gave three short bursts on the doorbell. There followed excited cries and clamouring feet as three of his children raced down the stairs and wrenched open the door.

Eager faces and scrabbling hands were what he was greeted with, and he was prepared to take any kind of risk for this. His children were crying out 'Dad! Daddy's here. He's here!'

Dan, aged eight, Ella, ten, and Martha, twelve, swung on him and pulled at him in their excitement. Only their six-year-old brother Tim was missing. He knew where the youngest would be, up in his bedroom, which was like a sickroom. Bob hugged the kids with equal enthusiasm as they clambered over him and dived into his coat pockets and the bags he had brought. He tried to pick all three up at once to swing them around but lost his balance and crashed on to the hall floor, with them piling on top of him, laughing. 'C'mon,' he said and jumped up and ran up the stairs, the children chasing after him.

Neither mobiles of dinosaurs and drones, the pop posters nor the colourful décor could disguise what Tim's little room had become. Their six-year-old was in bed, wheezing and rasping as he grasped at breath. He was small for his age and his illness, along with the medical paraphernalia which helped keep him breathing made him seem even smaller. His worn-out and anxious mother Kim was at his bedside almost trying to breathe for him, every one of her thirty-three years etched into her otherwise beautiful face by worry. She looked round and her anxiety deepened. Bob stepped over to the bed and put his arm around his wife and kissed her.

'Is the new medicine helping?'

Kim shook her head fractionally. 'You're taking a risk coming here this time of day.' That was causing her more anxiety, Bob knew, but he was determined to support her and be with his family over Christmas.

'Tim? Dad's here,' he said with cheerful expectation. 'How you doing, champ?'

The little fellow turned around and struggled to sit up. At

once Bob reached out to assist him and took over from Kim rubbing his back. It seemed to help briefly. Trying not to add to his wife's anxiety, he chose to remain ever optimistic that the medics or someone would find the solution to what ailed their son. None of the drugs and alternative regimes they had explored so far had helped him much, if at all.

'What if the police were to show up? It would be just like them to come over the holiday.' Kim turned away from her son, trying not to allow him to see her worrisome expression.

Reaching out to her, Bob pulled his wife close, wanting to give her both comfort and reassurance, knowing inside she was crying. He gently shushed her and kissed her on the forehead. Rarely did she allow the children to see her tears. Perhaps after the holiday he should turn himself in, but so far, he had resisted the notion as he sought evidence to prove his innocence. He knew he didn't betray anyone, only his family by staying on the run.

'Guess who I saw today, Tim. Can you guess? Well, it was Father Christmas.' Suddenly Eddie Scarr was back in his mind's eye, reaching for him and he couldn't find a happier image of Santa Claus. Scarr managed to put a negative spin on everything he touched. 'Right there with him was Luke Skywalker and Roe Dameron –'

'And Rey –' Tim struggled to say.

'That's right. They were giving out presents and they remembered you especially –'

Barely hanging on throughout this, a stifled sob escaped from Kim as she hurried out of the room. Bob glanced after her, but decided to leave her now and continued rubbing Tim's back, encouraging him to breathe slowly rather than snatching at breath as he was. 'It's okay, Tim, just take it nice and slowly like the lady at the hospital showed you. In . . . out . . . ' slowing his own breathing. Ella came and leant on her dad, putting her arms around him. He enjoyed that.

'He couldn't breathe at all earlier,' she said. 'Mum got really worried and was going to call the ambulance.'

'We don't need any more hospital visits for now, El, the danger's passed. He's going to be just fine, promise.' Did she believe him? Did he even believe it? He would keep praying and hoping for a miracle of some sort. 'We're all going to have a fabulous Christmas, like I promised you.' So easily did he make such promises to his kids, but he was determined to fulfil them. He turned as Dan joined in and poked his head under his dad's arm.

'He's not going to die, dad, is he?' There was real anxiety in his voice. 'A boy at my school died last Christmas.'

'No, Jesus won't let that happen, not to someone as nice as Tim. We'll go to Midnight Mass and say a special prayer for him.'

'Dad . . . Is it Christmas yet?' Tim asked in a little voice.

'Almost, Tim. You can open some of your presents, if you like.'

'Oh, can I open some of mine?' Dan said eagerly.

Always one ready to follow the rules, Ella said, 'No you can't open any until Christmas morning – anyway, dickhead, you haven't got any –'

'Nor have you, crap-face,' came the sharp response and they got to pushing each other. Bob knew this was a discharge of the tension his children were experiencing and he was the cause of it. He pulled them on to the bed and reached out for Martha, who had come into the room and remained silent, but who carried as much worry as her mother almost, along with doing a lot of the caring for Tim.

Later, in the kitchen where Bob found Kim, she was angrily throwing food into pans on the stove. She stopped and tensed when he stepped in behind her and began massaging the tight muscles in her neck and shoulders. There was no immediate response from her, nor was there any sense of rejection, which he optimistically took as a goodish sign.

'Everything's cool, Kim. I promise.'

Wrong note. Now with a clear rejecting shrug, she said, 'You're very free with promises, Bob Carter. Nothing's cool. You leave the house and Tim gets worse. And when you leave, we never know if or when we'll see you again, or if we'll have to move again or if we'll be seeing you on visiting days in prison. It's not fair to the children, or me, or you.' The words came tumbling out of her in an angry tirade. Christmas was always a stressful time for parents and his current situation was only making it more so.

Was he being selfish carrying on like this? Or was he simply being a coward, wanting Kim to tell him to turn himself in and end the cat and mouse game? Telling himself it was for the children was only partly true. It was for him as well; he couldn't bear the thought of being without them. He turned his wife to face him and lifted her chin and kissed her; then they were in each other's arms like nothing was amiss, with Kim's body softening.

'I'm sorry, Bob. It's been a really crap day.' She threaded her arms around and kissed him back.

Bob laughed and relaxed. 'It could have been worse,' he said casually. 'I ran into Eddie Scarr in the market.' Another wrong note.

'Oh God, then you shouldn't have come here, you shouldn't have.' All the tension flooded back into her body and that mask of anxiety dropped over her face. 'You've got to go – go now, please –'

'I promised to take Tim to the healing mass tonight,' Bob reminded her, but was unsettled by her reaction. Still he tried to reassure her. 'Scarr won't come here tonight. Not tonight, Kim, I promise.' There! That easy promise again. He didn't want to leave his family.

The second eldest of his children who had walked into the kitchen to hear part of their conversation, said, 'Who won't, dad?' Clearly thinking this was about Christmas.

'You worked with the wretched man. You know what he's like. Christmas means nothing to him,' Kim argued. 'It's just the sort of time he would show up. Please leave, Bob. Now, while you can. We can meet you tomorrow away from the house.'

The urgency of her appeal left him in two minds about staying, and he was coming down on the side of running like a thief when Ella said, 'But he promised to be home with us. You promised, dad –'

'Do you want your dad to spend Christmas in prison?'

'I hate that man, I hate him – I wish he was dead.'

'Come on, El,' Bob said calmly, taking his daughter in his

arms. He didn't want her hating anyone or wishing them dead. 'Everything's cool, El, promise. Even crabby old Eddie Scarr – can you believe I saw him actually having a snowball fight in the market earlier?'

A surprised Kim stood back from them in disbelief. 'I don't believe it. Are you sure it was him?'

'I've worked with him long enough. Well, it is Christmas, after all. Even Eddie Scarr might be affected. He can change.'

'Not for the better,' Kim said fiercely.

'Who knows, even him? Miracles can and do sometimes occur, especially at this time of year. Let's not worry about him and see what happens.' He put his arm around Kim and pulled her into his embrace with Ella. That's where he wanted to be, with his family, not dodging this nemesis he had brought forth.

It was a result. The pleasure most of the strike force displayed could have rivalled football fans when their team won against all the odds. Taff Thomas came out of the sweatshop office bearing a cheque like a trophy. He headed for the stairs; none of them could wait to get gone and back to what was on their mind: the party. He flapped the bank draft at Scarr.

'£48,011.58p recovered, Eddie. Result. You can't complain about that.' The hum of the sewing machines was starting up behind him. Scarr followed him and snatched the cheque.

'Talk to the bank – make sure there are cleared funds to cover it.' There was no way that could happen until after the holiday and Scarr was convinced that Kraske was scamming them. He had wanted a bank transfer, but the sweatshop owner couldn't remember his passcode. Which meant this whole operation could close down and disappear before the bank next opened for business. Trust no one to be honest or truthful, that was Scarr's credo. He sneezed, blasting out more germs, his cold not abating at all, despite this apparent result along with the various medicines he was taking.

A diminutive policewoman came through the street door ahead of several small round policemen. 'Bless you,' she said cheerfully as if entering into the Christmas spirit. 'You've got some illegals for us.'

'Glad to see someone's working aside from us,' Scarr growled. 'A woman with three young kids – Mrs Achebe. Not fit to be a mother, bringing kids here. Plus nine others we identified.' He went on down, passing the police officers on the narrow stairs.

The policewoman turned back. 'Oh, I say, Father Christmas, could I have a Barbie Doll?'

The policemen laughed and Scarr gave them a black look, sneezing again as he went out into the cold night.

Chapter 3

THE PARTY WAS UNDERWAY and looked like going on all night, despite some of the strike force members having families. They were splashing booze into paper cups like prohibition was fast approaching, while stuffing slices of pizza into their faces, buoyed up by the successful raid they were now all taking credit for. Still wearing his Father Christmas suit, Scarr came through the cheap offices with a sheaf of paperwork, tying up the loose ends with a report on the working claimants to be pursued after the holiday. If he didn't immediately capture the details on paper, some would be lost. At the very least he'd get those working claimants' benefits stopped and possibly the offenders sent to prison. He felt no compunction about doing this and would have preferred that the raids took place over the holiday, but none of his colleagues were up for it.

'What's that, Eddie?' Mike House said, his words slightly slurred with alcohol. 'Fixing up another raid for Christmas day?' He laughed at this comment, louder than it warranted and some of his crew joined in.

'Hey, Eddie,' Taff Thomas said around a mouthful of food, 'where d'you get that outfit? Oxfam?'

'He probably mugged the old boy outside Selfridges,' someone else put in, bringing more laughter. Until one of them started to choke on his food, which caused a moment's respite.

Scarr ignored their remarks, choosing not to give them the satisfaction of answering back; they were dossers after all, every one of them. Instead, he sat at his desk and began computing figures from today's raid, at once seeing something wasn't quite right. What else would he expect from this lot at Christmas? It looked like they were trying to give the sweatshop owner a Christmas present.

The teasing hadn't stopped, Mike House still leading it. 'About the only time Scarr would ever be welcome was coming down the chimney, dressed like he is.' More laughter rocked the room.

'While you laugh, we came up light, Taff,' Scarr announced in a sober tone, and sneezed again. '£7,201.07p surcharge should have been levied.'

'It was still a good result, Eddie,' Belle Moran said, coming out of her office to get some food and a drink.

She kept herself apart from the teasing, and mostly tried to defend Scarr's stance. Not that he needed her to do that. Better she didn't do this, but got after her shambolic crew instead, like the supervisor she was. Scarr never thanked her for her defence and often found fault with her work.

'It should have been better,' he complained. 'Why let any of these cheats off anything?' His foot hit something bulky under his desk, causing him to jump out of his chair. He pulled out a red sack – the surprise Taff Thomas warned him about earlier. 'What's this? A bomb?'

'Wouldn't that be about right, you misery guts?' Mike House said. 'It's presents, Scarr. Those things people give each other at Christmas.'

Unimpressed, Scarr heaved the sack on to the desk and opened it. He shook one of the wrapped boxes, which rattled. 'Sounds like a waste of money.'

'They're for the children's ward at the local hospital,' Belle told him.

'You got elected to deliver them – on account of you having nothing else to do on Christmas day,' Taff Thomas said.

Unmoved at the prospect, Scarr shook his head and said, 'I'm planning another raid. Someone special.'

Suddenly sobering, Mike House was aghast. 'You gotta be kidding!' He at once appealed to his supervisor. 'Belle?'

The look Scarr gave said he was deadly serious, regardless of what his supervisor had to say. He made most of the running anyway. In fact, Belle didn't say a word as more strike force members turned to her for an explanation. Scarr hadn't told her his plans for Bob Carter. He collected some soap and a towel from his desk and slammed the drawer and headed out to the washroom.

Whatever was in the glue he had used to fix his white whiskers, it wasn't coming off easily. Standing at the less than pristine basins and pulling at what remained of his beard was a painful struggle, his cold making his face particularly sensitive. He ached all over and wanted to get home to bed and shake off whatever was ailing him. Maybe it was flu or something worse. Worrying about his health wasn't usually a preoccupation and he took another swig of Benylin with some paracetamol. Glancing through the mirror, he saw Belle enter bringing two glasses of whisky and a small wrapped present, which she put on the adjacent basin. He hoped that wasn't for him, but guessed it would be. He hated receiving presents as much as he would giving them, were he ever to give them.

'We've had a good year,' Belle said and offered him one of

the drinks. 'thirty per cent better than the target. You're forty per cent over your personal best.'

'The year's not out yet, Belle.'

'Take tomorrow off, get some proper rest. You look awful – and those'll wreck your liver, Eddie –' seeing him shake out more paracetamol from the box.

What was this concern for his health about? Probably worry that her unit might not stay the top recovery strike force in the country. He met her look over his glass as he swallowed the tablets with the whisky, deciding to share who he'd seen earlier. 'Bob Carter's back on the manor. I saw him shopping in the market.'

Belle was surprised. 'Did he see you?'

'I got after him, but he gave me the slip. Then he always was a slippery toad. I plan to raid his house tomorrow.'

'C'mon, he'll be long gone.'

Scarr shook his head and sipped more of his whisky. 'He's a sentimental fool. He won't miss Christmas with his kids.'

'But he'll be expecting you.'

'We'll make it nice and early, Belle,' – still feeling bitter over what Carter did. 'I hold him entirely responsible for Jake's death.'

'Mm. Bob was very popular. Don't you think you should give yourself some ease? I do.'

'Jake was a great compliance officer,' Scarr said. He rarely complimented anyone, but his late partner was the exception. 'He knew how to spot the trickiest scroungers, even before they ripped us off.'

'He had a good teacher.' She hesitated, like she didn't want to broach what was coming next. 'None of this lot will volunteer, not on Christmas Day.'

'You could order the raid. It's done then.'

Still she hesitated. Scarr knew she was almost as sentimental as Bob Carter. 'I'll call Inspector Clarence,' she said, avoiding his look. 'The police can pick him up – after Christmas.'

'No,' he said firmly. 'Look at me, Belle.' He waited until she turned her soft grey eyes in his direction. 'I think I caught sight of Aram Guli at the sweatshop when I was chasing Carter. I want the satisfaction of putting the locks on both of them –'

'That was the problem before!' The words exploded out of her, surprising them both, causing each to take a step back. 'No matter what you do, Eddie, it won't bring Jake back,' she continued in a calmer tone.

Anger banged around in his thick head, making it ache more and still he refused to let this go. He didn't want to argue with Belle, needing her to order his colleagues to sign up for the raid. 'Jake and I identified Guli trafficking illegals – wasn't it Bob Carter who set us up?' He wanted to believe that and didn't know why he was now questioning it.

'Come on, we don't know it was for sure.'

Scarr laughed without any mirth and started to cough; then when it abated, he took a swig from the bottle of Benylin. 'Jake could be pretty ruthless, but he trusted someone he shouldn't have trusted. It was stupid. I thought I'd taught him better than that.'

'Perhaps he had a little more humanity than you imagined, Eddie.'

'Fine, but it cost him his life.' He swallowed the rest of

the whisky and slammed the plastic glass back on the basin, grabbed the towel and strode through to the showers, determined not to show how rough he felt.

That surge of anger from Scarr left Belle a little breathless and disappointed. She had hoped to reach out to this man, especially now, still confused about her feelings for him. It seemed there was no reaching out to him, nowhere he might come to meet her, but she refused to give up on him, even though he sorely tried her charity. She saw the little present she had offered him sitting on the basin and glanced towards the showers, wondering how it would be if she took it through to him. She picked up the box and hesitated. No, she had taken enough of Scarr's recalcitrance for one day. Now she had to face her crew, some of whom would be getting drunk.

Leaving the box on the basins she went out.

There were groans from the rapidly sobering strike force members when Belle claimed their attention and told them the plan.

'C'mon, Belle. Not on Christmas day,' Taff Thomas said. 'You don't want to work tomorrow any more than us.'

'You know what you signed up for,' Belle told him. 'Scarr's right. It's the best time to nab Bob. He wouldn't miss Christmas with his kids. He loves it.'

'So do we. Some of us have kids, too.'

'This is Eddie Scarr's personal vendetta, that's all,' Mike House stated emphatically. 'Let him do it rather than spoil everyone's day.'

'There's a little matter of honour here, Mike. Jake was his partner. How would it be if it was your partner?'

Looking round at Taff Thomas, Mike House said, 'It would at least stop him yattering on about bloody Millwall all the time!' That got a laugh.

'You must ask yourself why Bob fled as he did?'

Stumped for an answer, Mike House said, 'Well, I don't know. Perhaps he was staying undercover.'

'Scarr thinks he went native.'

'Bob was a good man, Belle,' Taff Thomas ventured feebly, 'even if he didn't support Millwall.' That brought an equally feeble laugh.

'Scarr's better,' Belle said firmly. 'Draw straws. I want two of you accompanying the police tomorrow – and no calling in sick.' With that she turned and walked into her office and slammed the door. The party over. How would she tell her mother and Teddy that she had to work tomorrow? All she knew was that they would be as disappointed as she was.

Chapter 4

HOT WATER POURING OUT of the shower head and deluging him didn't make Scarr feel one bit better, nor did he did imagine it would, no matter how long he stayed there. He was burning up with fever and reluctant to step out into the cold room.

Finally emerging from the shower to finish his whisky, he remembered he'd already drunk it and saw Belle's unfinished drink. Next to it was the present she had left him. He picked up the box and was about to open it, but put it down again, deciding not to get involved with present-giving. A sentimental waste of time and money. Instead, he picked up Belle's drink and sipped it, tasting her on the rim of the glass. A moment of regret which he quickly dismissed. Something made him change his mind – he guessed what, that wretched regret – and, putting the drink down, he opened her present to him. In the box was a coat pin in the shape of a sheriff's star. On it was engraved, 'My Number One!' Briefly it brought a smile to his face, which felt like a stranger there. Why had she given him this as a present? There was a card that simply read, 'Belle xx', which gave Scarr pause, but he didn't want to think about what was past and what it might have been, and certainly wasn't going to waste another second regretting it. He realized he had shivered, and told himself it was on account of his cold, nothing else; so, simply swallowed the rest of her whisky and finished drying himself.

Carol singers were gathered outside the busy pub on his

route home as Scarr went into the adjacent fast-food takeaway. Those who weren't singing were jiggling tins in front of revellers and getting fools to drop money into them. They were still there as he emerged and a woman stepped forward and jiggled her bag at him. He stopped and gave her a questioning look, wondering how many of these people might be benefit scammers.

'We're collecting to provide meals for the homeless over Christmas,' she explained in the well-modulated middle-class voice of the educated.

Probably not a benefits cheat, but you never could tell these days!

'What about the rest of the year?' Scarr asked before starting to walk away with no interest in an answer. Only Ms Educated pursued him, hopping in front of him, clearly thinking he was a mark.

'But Christmas is an especially difficult for these poor souls,' she said.

'Isn't it for everyone? Maybe they should try working like the majority of us and quit scrounging.' Sneezing loudly and missing her sincere 'Bless you,' he stepped around her and went on his way.

Not twenty paces further along on his journey towards home and bed he saw a young woman sitting on the pavement outside a closed betting shop with a McDonald's coffee cup in front of her. A familiar beggar's accoutrement. This one was wearing only in a flimsy short-sleeved dress. She must have been frozen; he certainly was, either that or she didn't feel the cold. Perhaps she had somewhere warm to go to sleep, or she surely wouldn't survive this bitterly cold night. For a fleeting moment of charity he thought perhaps he should send her to the night shelter, but they would already be full and with people waiting on the steps, and she wasn't his problem anyway. If his nose hadn't been so congested it would have started twitching: benefits fraudster for sure. Curled up next to her was a black and white mangy-looking dog, doubtless begging, too. Maybe he was her night-time warmth. A slightly drunk man came out of the pub and stopped in front of her and tried to pat the dog, but couldn't make it without risk of falling over. Instead, he reached into his pocket and pulled out a £20 note and handed it to the girl with, 'Merry Christmas'. Scarr felt inclined to run forward and stop him, telling him that giving to beggars only kept them begging.

She was watching the man totter off on his way, then stared at the money and didn't notice Scarr's approach until he was standing in front of her, but the dog did and got to its feet as if ready to protect her. Scarr felt slightly relieved she had this protection and wasn't sure why.

There was a startled look on the girl's face when she glanced up.

'What?' she said defensively, like she expected him to take the money. 'He give it to me. He did.'

'You'll catch your death out here dressed like that. Why are you begging?' Scarr wanted to know, as if he couldn't guess.

'What? Yes, my parents threw me out, when I became vegan – they let my room,' the girl explained in a shameful whisper, which didn't impress him.

He sighed wearily, as if understanding the problem, but wasn't about to cut her a break. 'Well, I have to give it to you for originality, coming up with that explanation. You're on benefits. Right.' The words were accusing.

The girl looked him directly in the eye, which slightly threw him. Neither beggars nor benefit fraudsters in his experience could rarely, ever do that. The fact that she could made this one a professional scammer, he decided. Then her next statement startled him – he blamed his cold for the effect it had on him.

'What if I told you that unless you change your ways,' she said like a caution, 'you are going to die a lonely miserable death, mister?'

Staccato laughter stuttered out of Scarr. As hollow as he decided her words were, somehow they reached deep into him. Again he blamed his cold. 'Well, thanks,' he said, recovering himself, 'at least that's original, too! What's your name? The right one. Lie to me and you will have a room for Christmas – not at the inn or the stable, but behind bars. I want your correct date of birth, too.'

'I'm Rachel Voss. I was born on 22 May 2003.'

The details came out too pat for Scarr to believe they were true. Nonetheless he tapped them on to his phone, inexplicably worrying about what she had said to him earlier as he awaited the response. Why was that nonsense getting to him? The dog was sniffing at the food in his carrier bag. Scarr pushed it away with his foot.

'D'you teach your dog to beg, too?'

'He's not mine,' Rachael said conversationally. 'I think he's hanging around you, waiting for you. He seems to know you. I'm sure he'd like some of your takeaway.'

'Hah, he'll be lucky!' Information on Rachel Voss started to appear on his screen and it was as he suspected. 'Here we go then, scammer. You wanna think again, Rachel Voss?'

'It is my name,' she insisted, 'and it's my right birthday. It is.'

Despite wearying of this and now desperate to get home, Scarr refused to let go and walk away. 'Rachel Voss was claiming benefits all right. The only problem is she's dead.'

'But it is me –'

'So you're dead, are you -?' At that moment he let out a gigantic sneeze, which allowed Rachel to fly up off the ground and dive straight out into the traffic, leaving the £20 note behind. Recovering himself, Scarr looked around only to discover that the girl had completely vanished as if into thin air. How was that possible? However, her dog had gone nowhere. It was still sitting, looking up at him expectantly.

'What? You wanna tell me where to find her?'

At least it wasn't a talking dog! It simply lay down and put its paws over its head. A real beggar-dog trick! 'I know that look,' Scarr told him. 'I've seen it a hundred times from beggars like you. At least you're not claiming benefits!' He turned on his way to the bed he knew was beckoning, but he stopped, not knowing why, then turned back. The dog was still watching him. 'Can you do any tricks?' he asked, and waited for an answer. None was forthcoming, of course. 'I thought not.' He sighed again. 'I must be a sucker for soft brown eyes. Here – now scram.' Scarr threw the dog a chunk of his food and the mutt leaped off the ground and caught it almost the second it left his hand. Well, that was a trick of sorts.

Seeing the £20 note lying on the pavement, Scarr wondered

if he was imagining it, rather like the girl. But no, he found it was real enough when stooping and picking it up. What to do with it? The donor was gone. Then he heard the rattle of coins and looked round to the woman shaking her collection bag. Why? He had no idea, and she was as startled as he was surprised by his actions when he stepped back to her and pushed it into her hand. 'Bless you, you kind man,' she said, like she meant it. But Scarr was having none of it. 'S'not my money. I found it on the pavement,' he said and quickly turned on his way.

The wharf-side housing estate where Scarr had his second-floor rent-controlled apartment, despite being fairly modern, had a desolate atmosphere about it. Most of the dwellings had been bought from the local council at a heavily discounted price and subsequently sold by those former subsidised council dwellers, often to people who lived abroad, or rented to equally remote tenants.

On his approach across the wind-swept open area in front of the block, Scarr was coughing and wheezing and swigging from his bottle of Benylin, not noticing the dog who was now following him through the swirling snow. On reaching the entrance to his building he turned, startled by a noise from amongst the Christmas-came-early rubbish spilling from the large communal refuse bins. On investigating further he found someone lying between the bins on the packaging from a 55" television. This person seemed to be trying to get up and couldn't. A mean-looking, unshaven man of indeterminate age with dreadlocks. Jake Marlow! Scarr realized. He was lying propped up at a peculiar angle, blood from a chest wound matting on his shirt. With a slight tremor, unsure if he was hallucinating or not, Scarr stepped closer, taking uncertain glances from side to side, suspecting he might somehow be falling into a trap.

'Jake?' he said in a hoarse whisper, fear creeping up on him. 'How the hell . . . ? Jake Marlow?'

When he got close enough to shake this man by the shoulder, someone quite different from that of his former partner stirred: a drunk with straggly hair and red wine stains down his shirt front. He mumbled, 'Merry Christmas,' and Scarr felt foolish about his mistake. He looked at the half-empty bottle of medicine in his hand and thumped his head, as if trying to clear it. Why he bothered to haul this guy to his feet, he didn't know. Another effect of this wretched cold, he assumed.

'Look, you'd better move, friend, or you'll freeze to death out here.'

Steadying him, Scarr sent the man on his way towards the entrance to the apartment blocks. Not knowing him, or being familiar with his neighbours, he simply assumed this was where he lived. When he turned, he saw the black and white dog.

'Okay, I was stupid, giving you some of my food. That does not make us mates. Go and find some other mug to beg from.'

The dog sat in the snow and stared knowingly at him. But Scarr simply hardened his heart.

In the building entrance there was a notice on the lifts informing residents they weren't working. This had been the case for such a long time that a notice would be needed informing people to the contrary when they were eventually made to work again. It was no wonder there was graffiti on the lift doors. Scarr crawled wearily up the stairs, anticipating bed. As he emerged on to the second floor, an elderly eccentric woman, whose name he believed to be Mrs Turner was shuffling along the corridor towards him on arthritic legs, head bent in concentration and talking to herself. Glancing up and seeing Scarr, she immediately turned and scurried back to her apartment, unlocked it and went inside.

'You've got nothing I want, dear,' he told her.

The only response from his neighbour was her slamming and locking her door, followed by the rattle of the unnecessary door chain as that was put in place. This was a low-crime block with rarely any break-ins. The whole place looked like it wasn't worth bothering with; no flower boxes adorned the glassed-in walkways, only spools of dust collecting where the place was cleaned so infrequently, no one accepting responsibility for the common parts, not even the service cleaners!

Three locks were set on the door to Scarr's dwelling. He unlocked them all and entered the cold, unadorned apartment, then turned the locks once inside, checking twice that the door was secure. The bareness of the place was a reflection of the bareness of his life and he liked it that way. Nothing and no one that couldn't be got rid of in a blink; there was nothing to which he was sentimentally attached and his intention was for it to remain thus. No photos or paintings cluttered the walls, no comfy armchairs or thick rugs to soften life, not even a lampshade to take the edge off the harsh light from the naked bulb hanging from the ceiling. Going through to the kitchen with his carrier bag, he put the light out and turned on the one in the kitchen. He always put lights off and on as he moved from one room to another so as not to waste electricity. From the bag, Scarr removed his takeaway, with its plastic fork and the single bottle of beer he'd purchased. This he opened and swigged from to swallow two more paracetamol. He went out with the beer and his evening meal, putting off the light and crossing the passageway to the sitting room, switching on the light. Here there was a single hard-backed chair, a small table with a desktop computer sitting on it and a narrow sofa beyond it. Scarr paused for a moment and took out the tin star Belle had given him. A smile briefly crossed his lips as he read the inscription, 'My Number One' then dismissed the thought and the smile. Things past were best left there and not clung to.

Presents were strewn everywhere around the apartment that Belle Moran shared with her daughter and mother. Three female generations at times made life fraught, but mostly they all got along fine. The sitting room was warm with festive decorations and the comforting glow from the gas fire in the grate. Belle finished wrapping yet another present for her daughter and carried it across to the tree, which was really too large for the room. No one minded though, least of all Teddy. Most of this effort was for her, as much as Belle and her mother enjoyed the season. Kneeling to arrange the presents, one addressed to Eddie Scarr caught her eye. She picked it up and read the label like she didn't know the intended recipient. But then she wondered if she really did know him and a sad smile crossed her face. When Angela, her mother, came into the room she quickly put the present down, knowing she'd be raising her eyebrows in dismay, having identified every present there, and knew just what comment her mother would make.

''God knows why you bother with that man, Belle,' she said, right on cue. 'I wouldn't waste my time over him.'

Dodging the issue, Belle said, 'Is Teddy asleep?'

'She's too excited to sleep.'

'I'll go in and say goodnight in a moment.'

Angela started around the room tidying up, condemning Belle's untidiness with her silence. Belle could almost feel her mother's disapproval and shrank inside from it.

'You don't need to do that, mum. It'll be a wreckage tomorrow when presents are opened.'

'Look at all these,' Angela said, the familiar edge of disapproval in her voice, 'enough for twenty or more children. You spoil her.'

'Oh, and you don't, mum?' Belle poured herself some more wine, wanting to chill and not row with her mother.

'She's my only grandchild – the only one I'm likely to have.'

This old sore was being poked at again, the scab picked off not allowing any healing to take place with her well-rehearsed argument. 'Don't start that again, mother,' – hoping the use of her formal title would stop her.

'Find yourself a man,' Angela said, bitterness creeping into her words. 'One who treats you right this time and doesn't leave you in the lurch.'

That was directly from her mother's own life. Belle had had all the details told her over and over about how her father had gone off and left her for some so-called floozy thirty odd years ago. She had been on her own ever since, from her own choice it seemed to Belle. Her mother was a trim, well-presented woman who could easily have attracted a man had she wanted to.

'Where do I find this wonderful man?' Belle responded. 'Under the Christmas tree?' There wasn't an answer coming forth from her mother, so she changed the subject, feeling slightly relieved. 'I may have to go back to work for a couple of hours,' trying to prepare for the shock of her working tomorrow.

'It's Christmas Eve.' Her mother sounded dismayed. 'You should be out having a good time.'

As should you on this and all of your other lonely Christmas Eves, Belle wanted to say, but knew this could easily tip over into proper row. More families rowed around this time of year than at any other holiday. With the excuse for saying goodnight to her daughter, Belle simply walked away, knowing her mother would be rearranging the presents and checking out the one for Scarr, shaking it, trying to discover what it was. Why she had put a present under the tree for him, Belle didn't know, as the likelihood of him coming here for Christmas was so remote. She supposed she wanted to find some good in Eddie Scarr, and believed it was there, but it was so deeply buried it would possibly never surface without a lot of help.

Chapter 5

Eating his takeaway dinner from the tinfoil container, Scarr logged on to his computer and, as he waited for it to boot up, his eyes trailed idly around the bare sitting room. The sparseness of the place offered him little physical comfort, but some satisfaction in knowing he was unencumbered and could up sticks and leave at a moment's notice. Not that he had any intention of leaving or had anywhere else he wanted to be. This place suited him nicely. The computer sang its one note so he paused from eating to tap a number into his phone, then linked it to his computer.

'Entry code: ZEON9/569/24,' he said. 'Edward Scarr.'

'Go ahead, Edward Scarr,' the disembodied voice replied, Scarr not being able to tell if this was a bored person or a computer-generated voice.

'I need the latest profile on Robert 'Bob' Carter. Date of birth: 19 May 1990.'

'This will have to wait till after the holiday. We've shut down.'

That incensed Scarr, who began to cough. Then, recovering, he said, 'The DCI computer never shuts down. Not like you slackers.' He coughed some more.

'You sound like you should be in bed, friend.' Now Scarr assumed it was a person speaking to him, not an AI response. 'Don't you know it's Christmas?'

'Not for half the world,' he argued. 'C'mon, I'm organising a raid on a dangerous criminal tomorrow.'

'Well, you'll have to access the information remotely. Your code will be – have you got a pen? – D-Delta, I-India, 9401/ AjaX.'

'Thanks for nothing,' Scarr said and rang off, then sneezed as he typed in the code between bites of food. He typed in Bob Carter's details and at once information started to appear on the screen. He sneezed again, wondering if he shouldn't get some rest and do this later. No. He decided to get it done now and sleep later. He glanced down to get a little more food and when he turned back to the computer screen, Jake Marlow's details were up there.

'Jake!' he said, startled. 'How? How did you . . . ?' Over his surprise he sighed and thought about his former partner, his instinct for spotting scammers and then putting the locks on them. He was rigorous in the pursuit. 'Ah, Jake, I still miss you, my friend. I don't know how you're up here. I thought I'd put in Bob Carter. Perhaps I'm going doolally. I wouldn't be surprised with this cold.' He stared long and hard at the picture of Jake, as if mesmerized; then he blinked and shook his head. He looked behind him but wasn't sure why. There was only the blank wall, one that could use a fresh coat of paint but wasn't likely to get it.

Turning his attention back to the screen, next he found it was clear and wondered what was going on. Hitting a few keys, he attempted to get Jake back up. Was he there in the first place? He was no longer certain. Nor could he get up the details of Bob Carter. What was going on? He examined the packet of paracetamol tablets he'd been eating like peanuts. Perhaps he shouldn't have been taking them with beer. The bottle stood empty by the computer, but he didn't remember drinking it. He shook his head again, and as he did so the whole building shook. Was it an earthquake? It felt like it, or as if it had been struck by a Godzilla-like creature. Then the light flickered and went out. There was a simple explanation, he was sure: either the bulb had blown or there was a power cut. In the darkened hall he tried tripping the light. No light, so he opened the small cupboard on the wall and using his phone light he checked the circuit board. Nothing there had tripped.

A violent hammering at the door startled him, causing him to turn in slight alarm it was so thunderous. He wasn't expecting a visitor and no neighbours ever called. His mind leaped to the possibility of it being someone he had sent down who was now seeking revenge. The hammering became so explosive he feared the door might burst in. Cautiously he started along to the hallway, collecting the baseball bat he kept for just such situations as the battering grew ever louder and more violent. Yes, at any moment whoever it was would burst the door off its hinges, he was sure. Then it happened and he raised his bat as the fearful rending ripped the door clear out of the frame, flattening it on the floor. Scarr took a swing at the familiar figure that dragged itself through the doorway, weighed down by what looked like a huge industrial doormat of personnel files. There were hundreds of them, so many that the figure of the man could barely move without loose pages falling from the file clips as he came towards him. Swinging the bat again and again, Scarr was dumbfounded when the blows simply passed through what he now recognized as Jake Marlow after some pages that were masking his face fell away. Worse was to come.

This apparition pushed right on through Scarr as though he was himself made of some sort of vapour.

Jake went on along the hallway and into the sitting room, leaving Scarr rooted to the spot and trembling so hard the baseball bat fell from his hands. Afraid to approach the sitting room, he waited, staring at the strange light spilling from the doorway. This was his imagination playing tricks on him, and he easily convinced himself of that when he turned to the front door and saw it was intact. To reassure himself he stepped up to it and checked the locks and hinges. Sure enough, they were sound; however, this did serve as a reminder to strengthen the hinges, as they were definitely the weakest point. He turned and looked along the hallway. The grey light was still there. The computer, of course, that was the light source! Even so, just to be confident of his next move he cautiously retrieved the baseball bat and crept towards the sitting room.

Springing around the door frame, Scarr froze, with only his jaw moving in spasm as he emitted a strange, frightened animal noise. Finally he was able to shape this noise into words.

'Oh dear God,' he mumbled barely coherently, 'I'm done for. I've wrecked my liver. I have . . . '

There was Jake Marlow standing in the middle of the room with his mat of files which was reaching down to trail on the linoleum floor covering. He was speaking, but no sound was coming from his mouth.

With a shaky voice, Scarr managed to say 'I can't hear you, Jake. I can't . . . ' He stopped abruptly. 'What am I doing? Talking to an hallucination.'

Jake slowly shook his head and pointed to the computer.

Puzzled, Scarr cautiously slid around the edge of the room to look at the computer as it obviously meant something to this apparition. Maybe it would give him some clue to what was going on here. Not for a moment did he take his eyes off Jake, who stepped forward, continuing to point.

'Stay back, stay back,' Scarr warned, raising the bat, 'or so help me, friend or not . . . ' A quick glance at the screen showed it now bearing all of Bob Carter's details. 'This is all too weird, and all these files . . . ' He edged away and picked up one of the fallen pages and read, 'Ronnie Booker? What's this? We busted him last year. He topped himself before we got a conviction – a real sign of guilt!'

At that Jake stabbed more violently at the screen and the details there.

Now Scarr got a little excited. 'Bob Carter? Have you got something to tell me about him? Yes?'

Again Jake spoke and this time clearly with some impatience, but again with no sound emerging as he continued to waggle his hand at the screen.

'Sound! You want the sound turned up?' Scarr shouted excitedly. He wasn't usually this slow on the uptake – his cold was the culprit. But just as quickly his excitement died as he stepped back and paused. 'C'mon, it's a joke. Right?' To his surprise when he turned up the sound on the computer Jake spoke. Scarr's immediate reaction to this was that he was completely cracking up.

' . . . These were all forged with the lives of those I helped to ruin,' Jake was saying in his deep, accented voice.

Scarr laughed, not joyously for seeing his old friend, but

nervously with the sound dying in his throat. 'It's Jake's voice all right . . . No, I know what's going on, it's those skunks in the office setting me up. Either that or I'm suffering some sort of delirium from the medicines I've been taking? Unless you really are a . . . Jake would know better than anyone just how Bob Carter was involved in his murder.'

At that Jake let out an angry wail like he was experiencing his murder all over again; the force of this slammed Scarr back into the wall. When the wailing faded and he recovered himself, Scarr started to giggle, believing now that this might really be happening.

'Only you, Jake, only you could find a way to help me from beyond the grave. I knew you wouldn't let that miscreant go unpunished. Oh yes, you were even better at putting the locks on the criminally undeserving than me. God, how I do miss you, man. What a team we were.'

'Eddie, I've been here with you all the while, trying to help you –'

'Brilliant,' Scarr said, stepping up for more of this. 'We'll nail that rat Carter for shoving the blade into you.'

The apparition sighed impatiently. 'No, Eddie, it wasn't him –'

'Don't be a dink, Jake, of course it was him. He was well involved. He'd gone over to the dark side – more money to be made there, obviously. It was as plain as the nose on your face, you just don't wanna –'

'Shut up and listen, man – listening was never your strong suit –'

Still not listening, Scarr insisted, 'I'm not going to listen to rubbish like that. Just help me take him down –'

With a regretful shake of his head, Jake informed him that he'd lost all power to interfere in human travails, his only purpose was that of a messenger.

'Then what's the point of this?' Scarr wanted to know, going back to believing this was the symptom of some kind of delirium he was suffering.

'You continue not to listen, Eddie. It will be to your cost if you don't.' He paused and looked about as if seeing other apparitions that Scarr couldn't. Then he seemed to nod, as if acknowledging them. 'You are going to get three visitors before morning. Each can help you reveal your true nature, that dim light to which Belle still cleaves.'

'All I'd want them to reveal is who it was who stopped you, if not Bob Carter.'

'Expect the first an hour before midnight. The Ghost of Christmas past –'

Suddenly Scarr let out a huge belly laugh, now convinced this was some sort of hoax. 'Yeah, sure. I'm definitely being had. You're just some kind of hologram, of course, like that one what produced Abba on stage making them thirty-year-olds again. Okay you slackers, how are you pulling this off?' He ran to the computer screen and waved his hand in front of it, trying to interrupt what he believed was the light source delivering Jake's image. Looking up, he saw that image backing away and along the hallway. Scarr ran to the sitting room door in time to see Jake back out through the front door of the apartment.

'Wait. How do they do that? How?'

He ran along to the main door and unfastened all the locks

and pulled it open. No one was on the walkway and he stepped over to the balustrade and pressed his face to the glass. No sign of Jake below, only some kids and revellers sliding around in the snow.

Scarr sneezed and heard the sitting room door bang, then open and bang again. Wind, he assumed, only then noticed there was no wind. The light in the apartment flickered then stayed on. Rushing back inside, he slipped over on an unnoticed file that was lying on the floor, momentarily winding himself. Now realising this file was real enough for him to slip on, sweat began breaking out along his brow. Yes, the file seemed real, but as he reached out for it, his hand trembling beyond his immediate control, the folder lifted off the floor and danced ahead of him out of his grasp. Scrambling up, he grabbed for it and missed, only to see it fly into the sitting room and into the screen. Now he knew for sure he was hallucinating. Physical files couldn't enter a physical computer, not without first a lot of processing. A moment was needed for him to collect his thoughts when, to his amazement, he was drawn to the screen as if by some invisible thread.

The file, which belonged to Rachel Voss, now opened electronically of its own accord and all the details of her scamming life were there. 'No, I'm not having this. I'm not,' he protested loudly and continued to bang his head trying again to clear it before resorting to hitting the computer in frustration. Only Rachel's detail steadfastly remained on the screen. Reaching up the bottle of Benylin, he searched the label for any listed adverse side-effects, but remembered they were on the information sheet inside the box, which he had discarded without reading. Never once did he read pharmaceutical advice, nor instructions about anything else.

'Now think, Scarr. There has got to be a logical explanation for this . . . Did I black out momentarily and pull her details up instead of Bob Carter?' he asked, speaking his thoughts. 'That's easily checked.'

As he reached out to type on the keyboard, he sneezed loudly, then again twice in quick succession.

'You ought to do something about that cold, Eddie,' Bob Carter said with a distant but concerned voice.

Swinging between startled and alarmed, Scarr whipped round searching for the source of the voice. Those jokers in the office, he further tried to convince himself. Sure, if they could make a hologram of the dead Jake Marlow, they could certainly conjure up this one. Very clever, but not quite Bob Carter's voice, he decided. The current voice sounded like it was out on the walkway and was too tinny while Carter had a strong, tuneful voice that worked well in karaoke. He was often singing in the office like he had not a care in the world.

'You should really be in bed with a hottie,' the voice continued. 'But there's no time for that tonight.'

The voice seemed to be nearer now. Scarr turned to the computer in time to see the tiny figure of Bob Carter hop off the screen on to the table, causing him to shrink back and stutter to a stop.

When the power of speech eventually returned to him, he said, 'I am hallucinating – water, I need water to flush these drugs out of my system.'

He rushed out, still managing to switch off the light as he

exited and the one on in the kitchen. Filling a glass, he drank the water in big gulps, then filled another and drank that one straight down. Finally, he put his mouth to the tap and drank until he was near to bursting. That would do it all right and he sighed with grateful relief. However, on turning he found the full-sized Bob Carter leaning against a cupboard watching him.

A high-pitched nervous giggle which he couldn't control emerged from Scarr and still he tried to convince himself this was the work of those strike force clowns. 'It has to be,' he said without conviction as he backed away.

'That would be too easy for you, Eddie,' Bob Carter said as if he'd read his thoughts.

With his confidence gradually returning and his giggle running into a dismissive chuckle, he said, 'Yeah, yeah, and I suppose you're the Ghost of Christmas past?'

'Not quite. I'm here to show you your future.'

'Well, it's nice to know I've got one, unlike you. Tell you what, Bob, I'll play this game. You be the Ghost of the Future, and I'll be your rich uncle who sends you off on a long holiday.' He laughed now, fully confident. 'If I switch off the computer, you know what will happen – you'll disappear, sunshine.'

'Fine. Let's put it to the test,' Bob Carter invited.

That brought Scarr up sharply, his new-found confidence quickly fading as he shuffled around Bob Carter and went through to the computer and hesitantly reached over for the mouse – why was it called that, he thought irritably as he shut down. At first, he was uncertain about turning around, but told himself he was being stupid. There was no Bob Carter in the apartment. When he turned, he smiled, Carter wasn't there; he never existed other than as a figment of his fevered imagination, and in the morning that would have passed and he'd capture the dog for sure.

'Are you a good neighbour, Eddie –?' the familiar voice asked.

The voice, however it came about, visibly shook Scarr. He might have been a leaf trembling in the wind, ready to blow off the twig. There was Carter right behind him, forcing him to shrink back in fear yet again.

'A good friend?' he continued. 'A good father?'

None of these questions was he about to even attempt to answer, and a good father was never in prospect. Instead, he ran at this apparition in panic and tried to grab him, but his hands only grabbed air, making Bob Carter roar with laughter.

'So, let's hear you make your case for your membership of the human race. Anything good on the credit side?'

Feeling affronted by this criminal being so superior, Scarr leaned in to confront him, eyeball to eyeball – those eyes did look remarkably life-like.

He said, 'Nothing so good as when I help get you sent to prison.'

'I believe you're a vegetarian.'

'What's that got to do with anything?' Scarr said defensively.

'Well, one or two animals you've not eaten might appreciate you. Why anyone else bothers, I can't imagine. To tell you the truth, Eddie, I thought you might have been smart enough to let me short-circuit Christmas Past as well as Present and take you straight to the future.'

'Future?' Scarr said scornfully, 'I told you just a few moments ago, you don't have one. Jake was the best friend I had –'

'I don't think so. Even Jake thought you pathetic with your obsession with putting the locks on the less fortunate. He felt sorry for you, you being so friendless. That's why he was prepared to humour you and stick around as your partner.'

'Your treachery got him killed,' he argued, suddenly furious as Carter's words wounded him more than he wanted to admit.

'No, it was your stupid blind arrogance that cost Jake his life,' Bob Carter countered. 'You knew how dangerous that trafficker was, but you wanted the cred for taking him down. How stupid was that?'

'No, we had to go after Guli when we did,' Scarr said fiercely as panic tried to smother him like a blanket. 'He was moving his whole operation. We'd have missed our chance.'

'No, Eddie, he was tying up with an even worse Romanian outfit. If we'd waited, we could have grabbed them all. But you had to be the number one striker. So, you rushed in and Jake ended up dead.'

It was plain to see what this wretch was trying to do, Scarr decided: he was attempting to dump his rubbish on to him to justify his own wrongful actions. He wasn't having any of it. 'I promise you this, I'll take you down, even if I have to trade the trafficker's liberty to do it.'

'I'm sure that'll help you feel better about Jake. Look, switch the computer back on and let me show you what's going to happen,' Bob Carter said solemnly.

'You put it on, if you're so smart.' Scarr watched him slowly shake his head and he felt a sense of triumph.

'I can't do that, Eddie. I'm just a ghost-like figment of your fevered imagination. I can't move any physical objects. Nor will you be able to if you come with me. So take a chance, turn on the computer.'

There was a long moment before Scarr logged on, deciding to give the lie to this whole crazy episode. At once a video of Belle came on the screen approaching through their ratty offices.

'The price may prove too high, even for you, Eddie,' Bob Carter said on a fading voice as he began to disappear.

Chapter 6

WATERY SUNLIGHT STREAMED THROUGH the grubby office windows that hadn't been cleaned since last Spring and wouldn't get cleaned again until next Spring. There wasn't money to spare for such things and no one on the strike force seemed to notice or care.

Members of her team were all righteously ticked off that they had to come in on Christmas Day. Belle had ordered them all to turn up as no one had volunteered. She was angry, too, as she stormed through to her office, pursued by Scarr. Others on the team watched them sullenly, some of them still hungover from the previous night's revelling.

'My informant reckons Aram Guli and his new Romanian buddy is back.'

'Why couldn't this wait until after the holiday, Eddie,' Belle said and saw his unyielding expression. 'Look, give this information to the police. Let them take care of it.'

'Are you serious? All those dossers do is hide in the police stations when there's any real trouble confronting them. Now's the best time to grab this scum. Even rubbish like Guli enjoys Christmas.'

'No one here will go with you willingly.' She nodded through the door at the strike force members who were still following their row. 'They rightly want time off with their loved ones. We all do.'

Scarr turned and gave them a challenging look. 'Fine, I'll

take him on my own,' he said defiantly and started out. Belle flew after him.

'Stop right there, mister. That's an order.'

Turning back and stepping in close to her, Scarr said through clenched teeth, 'What I bring in keeps this little outfit.'

'But I run it. Remember?'

'I taught you everything you know.'

'But it was me who took promotion, who accepted responsibility. Look, I've decided, no one's going after Guli or anyone else. Not today, not until after the holiday.'

The measured look Scarr now gave the members of the strike force caused each of them to avert their eyes; Belle did the same as he glanced her way and felt bad about it. Scarr nodded slowly, like his mind was made up. He headed for the exit, ignoring Belle's 'Scarr!'

The door banged after him and Belle strode into her office, slamming the door, feeling equally angry about Scarr undermining her authority. After a few moments, when she had cooled down, she opened her door to speak to her strike force, but none of them would meet her look. Then she knew she had lost them, that Eddie was right.

'Guli is wanted in connection with stabbing one of ours.' She paused, hoping to appeal to their conscience. 'I can't order you to go . . . ' None responded so she turned back to her office, disappointed.

The ghostly figure of Bob Carter stepped past the members of the unit with the ghostly alter ego of Scarr, both passing unnoticed. 'Why is it you can't get a single one of them to go with you, Eddie?' he asked conversationally.

'I suppose they've all worked their maximum overtime,' Scarr said.

'I don't think so. Most would bust a gut to catch someone who killed one of their colleagues. Take another guess – look.' He indicated Mike House who violently slammed a filing cabinet drawer in his frustration, then opened it and slammed it again before grinning at Taff Thomas. 'Even Taff, who was about as close as you got to a friend has had it with you.'

'He's such a sad bastard,' Taff Thomas was saying. 'Numbers are all that matter to Scarr.'

Belle glanced out to them from her desk, then got up and closed the door, shutting them out. This didn't stop Bob Carter leading Scarr through the wall to watch her punch a number on her phone.

'Mum,' she said. 'It's Belle.'

'I know who it is,' Angela said sharply. 'Your name and picture come up on my phone. Where are you now?'

'How's Teddy?' she asked, avoiding the question.

'She's helping with the dinner. You said you'd be home.'

Reaching for the bottle of wine on her desk, Belle poured herself a drink. 'You'd better go ahead and eat without me. Something came up.'

'The same old story.' Her mother sounded as annoyed as Belle knew she would be. 'I expect that bloody workaholic has got you there still.'

'He's all right, mum. Keeps us on our toes.'

The files which Belle was distractedly scrolling through were being read over her shoulder with vague curiosity by Scarr.

'Women are amazing,' Bob Carter said, 'so loyal and long-suffering, even when men cause them so much pain and heartache.'

'I must have something going for me then.'

'Not really, Eddie. You wouldn't recognize kindness towards you if it poked you in the eye. Look.' With that he poked his finger in Scarr's eye, causing him to jump back.

'Hey!' Scarr reacted by lashing out at him angrily and missed. 'Why d'you do that? I thought you couldn't influence things physically.'

'Of course not. But we're not flesh and blood at present.'

'She trusted you,' Scarr said, 'and you went bent.'

'Let's see if we can find any evidence to either prove or disprove that.'

'Oh yeah. You might convince me like this, but things will look really different when we're back on solid ground,' Scarr told him.

'The one person who truly cares about you, and not for the captures you achieve, but for yourself. It's going to cost her everything, and you.'

'What, Belle you mean? What happens to her?'

He turned with a sense of foreboding as Belle grabbed her coat off the door hook, leaving her protective stab vest on the peg. She wrenched open the door and hurried away.

'She's so angry she's going to follow you into danger without her Klaver vest.'

'That's stupid.' Scarr was getting agitated now and was keen to go after her. 'Stop her. Do something.'

'Only you can do that, Eddie – but not in this incarnation.'

'How? How? What can I do –?' He was panicking now. Then he stopped and collected his thoughts. 'This is the future. Right? It hasn't happened. Does it? Does she get hurt, Bob?' He gave Bob Carter a beseeching look with 'Bob, please?' And when no response was forthcoming, Scarr plunged across to the open door and tried to grab Belle's protective vest. His hand went right through it, again and again, further frustrating him. 'Why can't I pick it up? Help me, help me pick it up.'

''I told you. We have no power to intervene physically in these circumstances. Afterwards you may not even remember any of this.'

That suddenly caused Scarr to freeze right through to the marrow. 'Bob, am I –?' He didn't finish the question, but raced out of the room, Bob Carter going hard in pursuit. After all, he was supposed to be leading Scarr through the future, not the other way round.

The messy collection of low-rent rooms with half an unmodernized kitchen and a single toilet housed too many dejected immigrants without any sort of security or comfort. All of them were illegals, all destined to be slaves of one sort or another, fast-food delivery drivers, sweatshop workers, hospital cleaners, all working for little more than board and keep. When Scarr and Belle crashed in through the flimsy door, several people started out through the windows.

Nothing and no one could prevent Bob Carter leading Scarr's alter ego into this scene of panic and confusion to observe the turmoil as the original Scarr shouted, 'No one move

– hands where we can see them! You –' pointing at a frightened looking man whose appearance suggested he was of Middle Eastern origin, 'Hands on the table, now. Where's Guli?'

The immigrants stared at him through blank, uncomprehending eyes, none of them responding verbally.

Scarr pointed to the tiny side office and mouthed, 'Belle.' She got it in one and crept towards the office, as Scarr said in a loud voice, 'Let's do this sensibly. Everyone to face the wall – c'mon, hands on the wall –' but he moved in Belle's direction as she threw open the office door. Smoke was slowly filling the room from paper burning in a metal waste bin, when without warning the sprinkler system started up; the rolling tub of lard-like Aram Guli was pushing a bag out through the small window and struggling to follow it. Being only half his size, Belle courageously rushed forward to stop him and drag him back. Too late, Scarr's alter ego started forward ineffectually screaming, 'No, Belle!' She couldn't hear him as a knife suddenly appeared in Guli's hand and was thrust into her chest, nor was the original Scarr able to prevent this as he whacked Guli with his baseball bat, breaking his kneecap. The high-pitched screams from the incapacitated trafficker drowned out the guggling sound Belle was making as Scarr went to her aid. The trafficking soldiers, seeing there was no back-up, ran, so too did some of the illegal immigrants, driven by their instinct for survival.

'Belle, speak to me – someone call an ambulance. She needs an ambulance. Someone, please,' he said to the now fast emptying room. Those remaining with no English looked on actionless as Scarr punched numbers on his phone. 'Belle, you're going to be all right, I promise. An ambulance is coming. We got that low-life Guli. You'll be fine, you will . . . '

'Your finest hour, Eddie, your kindest deed,' Bob Carter told his ghostly companion as he looked on helplessly, along with those illegals who hadn't run. They watched Belle open her eyes and give Scarr a wan smile. In pain she still managed to reach up and touch his face.

'Stay with me, Belle – help's coming –' Scarr promised hollowly.

'Eddie,' Belle said in a frightened, shaking voice, 'I can't see you. Please don't leave me.'

'I'm right here, Belle. I'm not going anywhere.'

There was a long silence as water from the sprinkler system shut off, which only left the sound of Belle's laboured breathing. 'Eddie . . . ,' she managed between gasps of air, 'did you ever love me?'

That caused Scarr to hesitate; Bob Carter turned to the other Scarr and said, 'The sixty-four-thousand-dollar question, Eddie.'

Water dripping down the original Scarr's face made it seem as though he was crying. Avoiding the question, he said, 'We can't wait for an ambulance. I'm taking you to the hospital.' He picked her up like she was a feather-weight and ran out with her.

On the hospital corridor, Scarr stepped in through the locked doors after Bob Carter to see himself pacing nervously as he awaited news.

'Does she live, Bob? Tell me. Does she?' he wanted to know.

'Here comes your answer,' Bob Carter said, and nodded in the direction of his alter ego.

The anxious Scarr awaiting news of Belle turned as a surgeon emerged from the operating room. He pulled off his mask, slowly shook his head, then cast his eyes downward. 'I'm afraid the blade had penetrated her heart –'

'Not dead – no, she can't be dead. C'mon, you people work miracles.'

'I'm sorry. Perhaps if we'd got her sooner . . . I'm sorry. Would you care to see her?' he asked, still finding it difficult to look at him, especially as Scarr was fighting tears and looked like losing the fight.

Ghostly Scarr looked round at Bob Carter for direction, and when his guide didn't respond, he turned back to his original self. 'Go on, be a man, get in there and tell her what you feel. Tell her.'

With a violent shake of the head at the doctor, Scarr said brusquely, 'I've got a murderer to deal with.'

That wasn't good enough, his alter ego thought, and again he turned to Bob Carter for an answer. 'Why doesn't the fool want to see her? What difference can a few minutes make? Guli's not going anywhere with broken kneecaps.'

On the corridor Scarr started to leave, then turned back to the doctor and said angrily, 'She was stupid – not wearing her stab vest.' He was shaking with rage at this injustice.

Reaching out, ghostly Scarr tried ineffectually to stop his original self from crashing out through the doors. ''Is that it? All I've got to say for the only person I . . . ?' At first, he couldn't say the word and tried again. 'The only person . . . ?

Still he couldn't say it.

Bob Carter helped him to get there. 'The only person you ever loved, Eddie? Is that what you're struggling with? It sometimes costs us dearly when we risk emotional involvement. There's often pain and sorrow, as well as joy.'

That caused Scarr to bury his face in his hands and lean heavily on the wall, hiding. There might even have been a sob from him, hard to tell with the noisy air-conditioning running.

'You're not done yet, squire,' Bob Carter informed him. 'Oh no. The future gets yet bleaker.'

An exhausted, distraught-looking woman Scarr's alter ego recognized as Belle's mother, Angela, who had never liked him, came from the waiting room with a young girl. He assumed Belle's daughter, although they had never met. They walked towards the exit in heavy silence.

'Yes,' Bob Carter said as if anticipating his thought, 'Belle's daughter, Teddy. I'm afraid she goes off the rails when she realizes that mum isn't ever coming home. She gets to be too much for grandma to manage. Finally, the old woman gives up even trying.'

'What sort of person does that?' Scarr asked indignantly. 'Where's the father?'

'Yes, what about him, Eddie? Did you ever consider the possibility?'

Shocked at this, Scarr started to laugh. 'Are you kidding? How is that possible? Belle never said anything.'

'Did you even give her the slightest hint that you cared?'

'This is crazy,' Scarr insisted. 'I can't be. Belle would have said something. She was never backward in coming forward with her opinions.'

'Before she went off on secondment, you had an affair with her.'

'It didn't last –'

'Well, the result did! A bright kid, who questions things beyond her years.'

Pride was edging into Scarr's tone as he said, 'Well, Belle was pretty smart.'

'Not in her choice of lover!' Bob Carter countered.

Scarr didn't enjoy this observation and turned sharply to his guide. 'What happens to the girl? What did you say her name was? What happens to her?' he said insistently, like he suddenly had skin in the game, and seized hold of Carter when all he got back was an implacable look. 'Bob, c'mon.' Still with no answer forthcoming, Scarr flew through the doors after grandma and the girl.

At the lifts, the girl turned and looked directly at Scarr without actually seeing him, and shivered. 'Oh gran, I've gone all cold, like there's a ghost here. Is it mum, d'you think? Is it?' She started to cry and Angela drew the girl to her. 'It's no one,' she said. 'There's no one for you to give a moment's concern about, lovey.'

'Yes, I'm here,' the unseen and unheard Scarr said. 'Just here – me . . . your . . . dad.' He waved his arms at the girl, hoping she might shiver again at the recognition, but Angela steered her into the lift, now sobbing herself.

Belle's apartment was no longer the warm, inviting place it once was. Instead, it had a depressed, uncared for look. Teddy was throwing yet another hysterical fit, stomping around and slashing ornaments off surfaces to smash on the floor. There weren't too many things left on surfaces for her to break. All the while Angela, who had aged badly, was staring blankly from the window like she was mesmerized by the rain that was falling in steady sheets. Tears were rolling down the old woman's face as she sunk deeper into her blankness, completely ignoring the girl's tantrum.

Scarr's alter ego waited and watched from across the room, feeling uncomfortable and not wanting to be there. He seemed to have no power to stop Bob Carter from dragging him wherever he wished.

'The old lady had a co-dependent relationship with her daughter and so overcome with grief is she that, on the anniversary of Belle's death, she suffers a massive incapacitating stroke. Teddy is placed in care as there is no other family member or friend prepared to take on such a troubled child. She's about the same age you were when you were taken into care.'

A bellow of rage and pain rose out of Scarr on being given this information. 'No,' he screamed and turned away to wipe his nose on his sleeve, trying to hide the sob that escaped from him. He wheeled round to confront his guide. 'This cannot be allowed to happen – it's just something that might happen, could happen, right?' The words tripped out of him in a jumble, but Bob Carter got them clearly.

'These are choices you make, the course your actions take us on –'

Jumping right back in, Scarr said earnestly, 'I can change, I can, Bob. What if I marry Belle and become a father to Teddy?'

'Just words, Eddie, they won't do it,' Bob Carter said sceptically. 'And what makes you think she'll want to marry you after the way you treated her? You'll need to show real change through sincere actions.'

'How? I did lov . . . I was affra . . . What actions? I'll do whatever it takes.'

'Finding someone who's got something good to say about you would be a start. Even that dog who offered you friendship you rejected.'

'I gave it some of my dinner,' Scarr argued feebly, knowing he had lost this. Then he remembered someone. 'Taff Thomas – he was always fair minded.'

His guide laughed and disappeared and Scarr found himself disappearing along with him.

Next, they were standing in a cemetery at Belle's graveside as her coffin was being lowered into the ground. The entire strike force was there along with Angela and Teddy, plus a load of mourners, many of whom he didn't know. Belle had been very popular and had lots of friends. Some threw a handful of earth on to the casket, others a single flower. He saw Taff Thomas throw a handful of soil, then glance across at Scarr, who was off a little way on his own. It wasn't a very friendly look, Scarr's alter ego noted from a nearby gravestone where he waited with Bob Carter.

'He's upset over Belle,' Scarr said hopefully to Bob Carter. 'Look, he's going over to offer me his sympathy,' – as he watched this supposedly friendly strike force member approach the original Scarr. Suddenly, he seized hold of him and shook him, wrenching him round as if to hurl him into the grave.

'You should be in there, not her, you miserable apology for a human being. You never learn about people. You never will.'

Mike House stepped up to them and grabbed Taff Thomas. 'Don't do it, Taff. He's not worth getting yourself nicked over. All he cares about is blaming Bob Carter, because he's jealous of his popularity. He knows Bob didn't go bent.' All the while Scarr did nothing to protest.

Now Scarr turned to Bob Carter and laughed in his face, scornfully, knowing just what this was about. 'You cunning rat,' he said. 'Do you think I'm stupid? Do you think I don't see this for what it is: an elaborate hoax to stop me coming after you.'

Depression came over Bob Carter, as heavy as a wet sack. He closed his eyes and shook his head, despairing at Scarr's intransigence.

Ghostly Scarr watched himself standing alone by Belle's open grave, staring down at the coffin as hands crept out of the grave and seized him and dragged him into the hole with it. He screamed and screamed.

Chapter 7

IN TOTAL TERROR SCARR threw himself out of the grave, screaming to be spared, promising to change, only to find himself not buried alive but on the floor of his apartment, drenched in sweat and trembling. Slowly he looked about himself and, realising where he was, felt deeply embarrassed. He didn't usually have scary dreams, not since the one he had had where he dreamed he was being attacked by a ferocious brown bear. Rather than waking himself out of the dream he had decided to confront it, punching it on the nose. Both the bear and the fear had disappeared. But he couldn't shake off the feeling ushered in by this dream as easily. The dark, damp grave clung to him like a heavy black shroud. Perhaps he should ring Belle and make sure she wasn't dead. That was stupid, he told himself, of course she wasn't dead. She would think him foolish for checking. This was yet another effect of his rotten cold which he was determined to get shot of.

Climbing up off the floor and seeing the Rachel Voss details on his computer screen, he felt hugely relieved. Of course, these were the details he had summoned earlier before all that nonsense with Bob Carter. His throat was dry and his head hurt and the one bottle of beer he allowed himself at dinner was empty. Not even a drop or two in it. He picked up the bottle of Benylin and considered taking a swig. Best not, he decided, and went to the kitchen for a glass of water instead.

Putting off the kitchen light and switching the one on in the sitting room as he returned, Scarr stopped dead, the glass sliding from his hand and smashing as it hit the bare floor. Rachel Voss glanced round at him from where she sat at his computer for all the world like it was hers.

'Ah, you're here,' she said briskly, 'good. We'd best get started. You've got a very busy day tomorrow.'

Overcoming his shock by clamping his jaw to stop it rattling, he finally got it under control sufficiently to say, 'Forget it. This has gone far enough. I need to get to bed and get some rest.' He looked down at the shattered glass at his feet. That was real enough, but it didn't mean this woman was. Yet now he found himself responding to her beckoning.

'Wait a minute. It's all coming back to me now. I busted you just before last Christmas. You were a working claimant.'

That seemed to throw her off her stride for a moment. 'Sure,' she said. 'Scrounger, you called me for temping – delivering letters for Royal Mail. I was just trying to get a bit of cash to go back home with some prezzies – so mum and dad wouldn't know how far down I'd slipped on the ladder.'

'I hear this sort of nonsense all the time. Every excuse every slacker ever came up with.' He shook his head wearily. 'This is madness, of course. You. Whatever figment of my blocked sinuses you are, lady, when I count to three and open my eyes, I promise you'll be gone.' With that he confidently closed his eyes and started to count out loud to three, but he was becoming less certain with each number. Cautiously opening his eyes and finding Rachel still present, he began to tremble again and tried desperately to cling to the belief she was caused by his cold or the remedies he'd taken, as his grip on reality began to slip and he felt himself plunging into madness.

'What do you want with me?' he finally managed to ask.

'You were told to expect me – the Ghost of Christmas Past.'

He tried to laugh dismissively, but what emerged wasn't substantial. 'Of course – I had on a Santa Claus outfit earlier today,' he tried feebly, 'but that didn't make me Father Christmas.'

Now Rachel laughed. 'That would take a lot more than a costume! Look, there are things from your past that made you like you are. You need to visit them. C'mon,' she ordered.

'All I need, lady, is a good night's sleep so those drugs I've been taking can do their stuff. I'm still hallucinating from them, I know I am.'

Lurching forward without warning, he suddenly slashed at her with his hands, trying to make her disappear. Again it didn't work, his hands went right through her. Someone once said that was a sign of madness: repeating the same erroneous action and expecting a different result, but he wouldn't accept that he was wrong here, or that he was entering madness. 'If it's not the drugs, it's them skunks on the strike force doing this.'

'No, we're all just trying to help you, Mr Scarr.'

'Like I need help. A man who's delivered 49 per cent better than his target; a man with a personal commendation from the Works and Pensions minister? I don't think so, lady.'

'You'll recognize this young person, of course.' She curled her finger then pointed to a young boy who appeared on the screen, causing Scarr to explode angrily and slash even more wildly at her. 'Leave him out of this.'

'But that's what set you on your current path. A frightened

and unhappy little boy. Come on.' She beckoned him to the computer.

At first Scarr resisted, refusing to look at the screen. Then when he did, at her insistence, there was nothing on it. This caused him to grow bolder.

'These things are best filed away and forgotten,' he said.

'Stubbornness is pointless and it won't help you to change.' She tried typing some information on the keyboard, but couldn't. 'I keep forgetting I can't do this anymore. I'll need your help,' she said, reaching out to him.

Feeling he could now take control of this situation, Scarr folded his hands under his arms. Only it did no good, for as she stared at him, he found himself acceding to her will like he had none of his own. I'm not doing this, I'm not doing this, he told himself over and over, all the while his fingers were moving across the keyboard, tapping in his own name and date of birth. The image of a seven-year-old appeared on the screen, tearful and frightened, as an older girl led him into a grim-looking reception hall of a big old house.

'Do you remember your first Christmas there?' Rachel asked.

'No – no, I don't.' Scarr shook his head violently as if to try to distance himself completely from the memory. He forced himself to turn away, trying to deny this unhappy chapter in his life.

'I'm not surprised you choose not to remember. You were so unhappy there.'

The madness continued for Scarr as Rachel caught hold of his hand and, despite his resistance, led him on to something he knew was impossible: across the table and up through the computer screen.

Grey paint on wooden panels and threatening shadows, he remembered, were the predominant features in the bleak hallway of this rambling house she had brought him to. And the ever-present smell of disinfectant. There it all was now as he stood with Rachel, watching the young Eddie Scarr, waiting with his sister, Franny, who was fourteen and wasn't being taken into care herself. The young Eddie was hanging his head in fear of what might happen to him without Franny, clutching in one hand a plastic carrier bag with most of his worldly possessions and in the other a piece of string to which his dog, Buster, was fastened. After a few moments, as if sensing his concern, Franny squeezed his hand and rubbed it in a grown-up fashion.

With a trembling lip, young Eddie said, 'I don't want to stay here, Fran. I don't like it. It smells funny. Please don't make me stay here.'

'It'll be all right, Ed,' she assured him, 'you got Buster with you. He'll look after you. Anyway, it won't be for long. Just till I get a job and get us a nice flat, then I'll come back for you. Promise.' Her words had a hollow ring.

Unconvinced, young Eddie said, 'No, please, Fran. I don't like it here –'

'It's just till I get a job and find us a flat,' she repeated with the same hollow ring. 'I will get us one, I will. Then I'll come back and get you. Promise –'

They both looked up sharply as a grey-looking, overweight Care Father waddled down the uncarpeted stairs. He was wearing a baggy, ash-stained cardigan and jeans that had been turned up but were still dragging on the floor behind his gone-over-on-the-back plaid slippers. Reacting with surprise on seeing the three of them, he addressed Franny. 'Where's his social worker? Not you, I know, you're not old enough for that. Who are you? We was only supposed to be getting one. And certainly no dog.'

'I'm his sister, sir. Social Services just give us the bus fare for me to bring him,' Franny explained quickly. 'Buster's his dog, ain't he, Ed.'

'Well, we certainly can't have no pets here, dear. Not here. There's no money to feed them or for vet bills. And what if everyone wanted a pet? No, he'll be fine here without his dog, won't you, son?'

There was no reply coming from young Eddie, who sunk his chin even lower into his chest to hide his tears.

'What do we call you, young man?' the Care Father said kindly. 'Edward? Eddie? Ed? Teddy? Speak up, son.' He cupped his ear with his pudgy hand when young Eddie mumbled something. 'Can't hear you. I can't hear you,' he said with emphasis. 'You'll need to speak a bit louder around here, son, if you want to be heard. Now.'

'I want to keep my dog,' young Eddie said defiantly.

The look that came over the man's putty face didn't bode well for young Eddie. Being quick to dangerous situations, Franny said, 'He don't want to stay here, mister, Eddie don't, nor his dog.' Her words didn't improve the Care Father's manner.

'Oh, don't he? Why's that, young Eddie, when everyone's so

very nice and friendly here?' Still with the same cross set to his demeanour.

Trying without success to take the string tied to Buster from his hand, she eased her brother forward. 'There, you see, Ed. It'll be all right. It will.'

'Of course it will, sister. He'll soon get used to our funny little ways and fit in just fine. Now you toddle along and take the dog.' He reached out for the string in young Eddie's hand, but Eddie withdrew it. The Care Father seized the boy's hand and wrenched the string from it, extending it to Franny. 'Take the dog and go. Come on, young Eddie, no more crying now, you hear? Bite your lip to stop yourself if you're about to cry. No one wants a cry-baby, do they? Leave now, sister. He's in good hands. Short goodbyes are the least painful, you know.'

Franny was about to kiss her sobbing brother goodbye, but glanced at the Care Father and stepped back, thinking better of it. She started out quickly dragging the reluctant dog. Eddie turned to watch them go. The dog looked back at him with big sad brown eyes, but his sister didn't turn in his direction again. Eddie sobbed louder as the door banged and they were gone out of his life.

Scarr stared after young Franny and was almost in tears as he turned to Rachel and said bitterly, 'This is stupid. What am I doing here? This has got nothing to do with anything.'

'Do you remember what you were feeling when that horrid man led you away?' the young woman asked.

This was too painful Scarr realized and shook his head, not wanting to remember but unable not to look as the Care Father dragged young Eddie roughly up the stairs.

'The quicker you find your feet here, sonny, the better for all of us. Stop that snivelling now, you hear?' He gripped him more firmly as young Eddie tried to wriggle free, wanting to run back down after Franny and Buster.

'Come on,' Rachel said like someone in complete command, and pulled Scarr up the stairs with her after them.

In one of the eight narrow beds under the sloping roof where a dormitory had been created, Rachel walked Scarr through to where young Eddie lay awake in his bed sobbing helplessly. Some of the other children were awake and peeking over their blankets anticipating what was about to happen, but none going to comfort or reassure him. Rachel watched him for a few moments as emotions raced across his face while bitter memories rose unbidden like spectres to haunt him.

'Your whole world collapsed in chaos when your dad committed suicide after your mum had died following an abortion,' she said quietly. 'All a boy of seven was able to make of this was that somehow it was his fault and so chose to blame himself.'

Scarr stiffened, tensing his body against this. 'Mumbo psycho-bloody-logical jumbo. They died and my sister just shoved me into care. End of story.' There was anger and a lot of pain in his response, like the terror this memory held lay just beneath the surface and was threatening to break through.

'Look at what happened subsequently. Night after night after night you cried yourself to sleep, waiting for your sister to return as she had promised. Only as far as you knew she never did.'

'That's right, she abandoned me and I couldn't have cared less. I didn't need her or anyone else.'

'Then why are you crying and disturbing everyone in the house?'

Before Scarr could answer her, the dormitory door was thrown open to bang against the rafter making the room shudder. The Care Father hit the door with the heel of his hand when it bounced back at him as he had done many times, then strode along the dormitory with his torch, its beam finding the culprit. Breathing heavily from exertion, he stepped up to young Eddie and caught him by the shoulder, shining the light in his face.

'Must we have this wretched crying night after night, boy? We can hear it right through the house. Stop it at once, I tell you. We don't want it. It's not necessary, is it? Do as I say and bite your lip.' This only caused Eddie to cry harder, and the Care Father to sigh heavily, at a loss to know what to do. 'Look, none of the other boys are snivelling like you. Just control yourself. Do like I said, bite your lip, d'you hear? Bite your lip.'

Eddie did as he was bid and bit down hard on his bottom lip, momentarily catching his breath and stopping his sobs as he tasted blood in his mouth. This seemed to satisfy the Care Father. He clicked off his torch and went out, closing the door.

As he watched him go, Scarr sagged in shame at his younger self for being such a baby. How could he have been like that? He tried to turn away from Young Eddie, who now began sobbing again, but Rachel prevented him leaving.

'Look, lady, I've got a really heavy day tomorrow. I've no time for this sort of nonsense,' he said, only he couldn't leave, it was like she held him locked in some kind of steel grip, yet she wasn't touching him.

The distant sound of someone thumping up the stairs was heard getting closer and finally the door flew open. A thin woman with the pale yellowish face of a smoker and the skin stretched over prominent bones, appeared and waited a moment trying to identify the culprit, as if she didn't already know who it was. She was known as the Care Mother. She strode over to Eddie's bed and wrenched the covers back, finding him shaking.

'Up. Up,' she ordered. 'Every night it's the same with you, cry, cry, cry. That's all you do. You'll give my husband a heart attack and put years on me as well. It won't do Eddie Scarr. Up, up. Come on!' When he didn't respond fast enough, she dragged him out of the bed and along the dormitory, past the other boys who were all awake now but pretending to be asleep, fearing this woman's wrath might turn without warning in their direction.

Showing more than a spark of concern now and against his better judgment, Scarr started forward after them. 'He didn't mean to, Care Mother' he said, keeping his distance rather than using 'I' in referring to his younger self. 'He couldn't help it. He was scared. He was.'

Stairs from the dormitory led immediately on to a dingy, dimly lit corridor with an adjoining corridor that ran at a right angle to it. Here a familiar door with a small window was where Scarr was drawn by the sound of a thrashing. This was the punishment room to which he was frequently taken. He peered through the window and saw the Care Mother whacking Young Eddie around the legs with a leather strap, her preferred instrument of chastisement. He felt a moment of pride that no sound of any kind emerged from his young self as the boy bit down hard on his lip, drawing blood, only the swish-thwack of the strap hitting his bare flesh again and again was heard. The Care Mother had pulled down his pyjamas to deliver this.

Scarr twitched uncomfortably with the memory as he now watched, steeling himself against that earlier spark of concern igniting into a flame of action, momentarily forgetting that he couldn't take action in this dimension. Suddenly aware that he was being watched, he turned to find Rachel on the corridor and said dismissively, 'Well, he had it coming for being too soft.'

'You learnt your lesson well, Mr Scarr.'

'Sounds good to me,' he said brusquely and started away. But Rachel darted in front of him, cutting off his retreat.

'Only you learnt too well. You buried your feelings so deeply that they might never resurface. And I'm afraid we're not done with the little punishment room. Look.' She pointed to the door and there was young Eddie's face pressed to the window, staring forlornly at the scene in the hall below. Children were swirling around a decorated Christmas tree, some with adult family members giving them little presents.

'You were the boy on the wrong side of the window, always looking in hopefully. You waited and went on waiting, and still Fran didn't appear, not even at Christmas. So, you protected yourself by learning not to expect her; then you learnt not to care or feel the pain of that bitter disappointment.'

'Why should I care?' Scarr said with a mixture of hurt and hostility. 'No one cared about me.'

'You're so wrong, Mr Scarr. Franny cared and didn't stop caring about you. She tried to visit you on several different occasions.'

The force with which Rachel said this stopped Scarr in his tracks, and he couldn't but turn in the direction of Rachel's curling finger.

In the drab entrance hall of the care home where the wilting Christmas tree was lying on its side, shedding pine needles, Franny waited expectantly as a boy in shorts charged through – not her brother. The Care Father shuffled through in his plaid slippers and shouted, 'Walk! Don't run inside, son.' Causing the boy to slow to a forced walking pace. With a smile as thin as his wife, he approached Franny.

'I'm afraid you've had a wasted journey again, sister. I'm sorry.'

'I couldn't come on Christmas,' she explained, 'I didn't have m' train fare.'

'No. He's back in the punishment room where all naughty boys get put.'

'Couldn't I see him just for a little minute, sir?' Franny pleaded. 'So I can explain why I didn't come.'

'Ah, you could, just for a little minute, of course, sister.' He paused. 'But on the other hand that wouldn't be punishment if we didn't keep to the rules, would it? If we don't keep to the rules, you must understand, everything breaks down. Then we'd have chaos, wouldn't we?'

On the verge of tears at this disappointment, she made one final appeal. 'Eddie's not a bad boy, sir. He isn't, really.'

'I'm sure you're right, sister, but we can't tolerate misbehaviour, can we? When your brother learns that, we can reinstate his visits, can't we? But not until.'

Franny started away, crestfallen, tears now leaking from her eyes. She went on leaden legs, but turned back, extending two bars of chocolate from her coat pocket. 'Will you give him these, please, and tell him I came to see him? You will tell him, sir?'

Without replying, the Care Father took the chocolate and went off along the hallway, unwrapping one of the bars.

Chapter 8

ENTIRELY AGAINST HIS WILL, Scarr's fingers moved across the keys of his computer, not understanding how a ghost-like figment of his imagination could make him do this. On the screen, information about his sister started to appear: Frances Scarr aka Delores Ross aka Dilys Wise and Debbie Dolittle, age forty-five; itinerant drug-pusher; benefits recipient; benefits fraudster, sentenced to two years in prison for claiming Social Security whilst working in a massage parlour . . . Scarr reached out and yanked the lead from the computer, causing the information to vanish but his shame to lessen not at all. It wasn't his sister's lifestyle that caused his shame but his part in what happened to her. He didn't want to revisit that.

'Someone has gone to a lot of trouble for you, Mr Scarr.' Instead of an impartial conveyor to significant events in his life, Rachel was now revealing considerable annoyance in her tone of voice. 'Some people seem to think you're worthwhile. I'm not sure why, but then I'm just one of those useless feeders, as you called us.'

'Just what is it you want from me?'

'I don't want anything. Not a thing – other than for you to plug the computer back in.'

Again, Scarr was helpless to refuse and did as she told him. At once the face of a prematurely old young Franny appeared on the screen and his heart sank, after feeling a little kind of palpitation which he didn't understand. Why was it happening when he almost didn't recognize this woman, and the very last thing he wanted was to go where Rachel was now leading him: a Chinese 'medicine' parlour as the massage joint was called. Here women of all shapes and sizes and ages were hurriedly pulling on Chinese robes over their skimpy, diaphanous costumes. Scarr and Jake Marlow, along with other strike force colleagues, moved amongst them, ignoring the protests of customers, some of whom were hiding under couches or trying to slip away unnoticed. There was no official interest in the punters, only the masseuses who were claiming benefits, which Scarr suspected was the majority of them. The proprietor of this establishment, George Zhong was protesting in some sort of pidgin Chinese mixed with English.

'We want the correct names, dates of birth, and the present addresses of all the practitioners working here,' Scarr was shouting at this man, which wasn't helping to lower the temperature.

'No work, boss,' George Zhong said flapping his arms like an overweight penguin trying to fly. 'No work here, not work.'

Scarr simply turned away, having no interest in listening to his nonsense when Jake Marlow came through the layers of curtains draped around the various massage tables and pulled him aside.

'Eddie!' he said with some excitement. 'The ol' tom on the front desk's got the same name as you. You got a sister by any chance?' He laughed nervously.

'Do I look Chinese?' Scarr said irritably, like he was caught out.

'Nor does she. She was probably a looker in her time.'

'Where is this person?' He knew he couldn't avoid the

inevitable and strode through and looked around, relieved when they found no one.

'She was here,' Jake said. 'I mean, if she was like, you know, related, we could give her a break – if you wanted to, that is.' He pulled back a heavy curtain that was closing off a cubby hole to reveal Franny sitting on a couch, her face buried in an Elle magazine. She looked up and gave Scarr a withering look, clearly recognising him. Scarr's lip started to twitch and he bit down hard on it, then quickly turned out to the street, where Jake pursued him. He caught hold of Scarr's arm and stopped him, not understanding what was happening, never having seen his partner affected in this way.

'What d'you wanna do about her, man? I mean, she must've been a bit of a looker in her time, Eddie,' he repeated as if that made a difference.

'If she's working and claiming benefits, treat her no different,' Scarr told him flatly, his lip now under control.

'But what is she – she's family, man!' suddenly getting it.

'And a possible benefits fraudster.'

'C'mon, man. We could pull her sheet and give her a break.'

Incensed now, Scarr suddenly rounded on him, causing Jake to step back. 'Is this Jake Marlow? The enforcement officer who learnt to be better than his teacher?'

Jake gave an embarrassed laugh. 'No one could get better than you at this game,' he said and laughed again, this one comradely.

'What would you do if she was your sister, Jake? Let her go? Is that what you're trying to tell me?'

Wrong-footed, Jake said, 'Well, it might help sort her out – I mean, we all done it, man.' He stepped back from Scarr's look and smiled. 'Well, maybe not you, Eddie.'

Back in his sitting room Scarr wanted to get away from his computer and this young woman who was causing him such heartache. Rachel had the irritating habit of slipping round in front of him to stop him and make him feel even more uncomfortable. Try as he did to turn away from her, she always managed to be there, always in his face.

'Do you know what happened to her after she left you in care?' She waited when he didn't answer. 'Weren't you just a little bit curious? After all, you thought the world of your big sister. Wasn't she always sticking up for you at school, fighting your corner?'

Not being able to run away from this young ghost of a woman, however she was here, Scarr clamped his hands over his ears, wanting this to stop, not wanting to know about Franny. But no matter which way he turned, the girl was back in his face, refusing to let him escape. He was getting more and more agitated, the cold he was suffering with feeling like it was about to overwhelm him.

'You had open access to police and Social Services records,' she reminded him. 'You could easily have tracked her.'

Enough was enough and Scarr now exploded as he rounded on her. 'Did she ever try to find me?' he demanded. 'She dumped me in that crummy care home, let my dog go. I was there for nine years. I never received a single visitor, never saw a friendly face or had a kind word said to me. You say she tried to see me, well, she didn't try hard enough –' Now the pain of those years was in full-flood and was set to wash him away emotionally and might have done so if Rachel hadn't come at him accusingly.

'Did you ever stop to think what might be happening to her, what her circumstances might have been?' she said. 'Instead, all you wanted to do was wallow in self-pity.'

'Whatever those circumstances were, they had to be better than mine,' he retorted, resenting her telling him he was being self-pitying.

'This was a vulnerable teenage girl living on the street, no roof over her head, finding shelter where she could, easy prey to men.' All sense of objectivity having vanished from her now, she was totally empathising with Franny. 'Look –' drawing him to the screen where the teenage Franny was now seen wandering the street at night, waiting to hook car drivers.

Again he tried to turn away and not look, but as Rachel pointed to the screen, once more he found himself powerless to avert his eyes.

The Citroën driver whose attention Franny managed to catch was a stern-looking, homburg-wearing, middle-aged man with penetrating, almost messianic eyes and a flattened nose that was indicative of an earlier boxing career. As if undeterred by any of this, she leaned down to the passenger window with a warm smile, knowing that a smile always helped her in such circumstances.

'Won't you get in, little lady?' he invited in a well-modulated, educated voice.

Scarr stepped across the pavement with Rachel to get a better look at this man, seeing his shiny black jacket, then his dog collar, which Franny clearly hadn't noticed. 'A bloody vicar! I've got a bad feeling here – who is this man really? He's dodgy, Fran. Don't get in the car, don't go with him –' He ran forward and tried to grab his little sister but couldn't get any sort of purchase on her as she climbed into the car. 'Help me here,' he said to Rachel, making her smile.

'I'm the Right Reverend Portland,' the man in the homburg said. 'You know why you are here –?'

With a slight tremor in her voice, Franny said, 'I think I made a mistake, sir, I did, sorry –' all her instincts now telling her, too late, that this man was dangerous.

'God has entrusted me to help you by expunging all your wickedness.'

In full panic mode, Franny was trying desperately to open the door but couldn't. Outside Scarr was trying to pull open the passenger door, but couldn't. As the car drove away, he turned helplessly to Rachel.

'Where are they going? Where? Take me.'

Again his response brought a smile to Rachel. Perhaps after all she was getting through to this seemingly unfeeling monster.

They arrived at the top of a wind-swept, multi-storey car-park, which puzzled Scarr. 'Why have you brought me to this place?' His question was immediately answered as the Citroën, driven by the Right Reverend Portland, turned on to the open top deck where only a few cars were parked. It stopped and Franny tried at once to scramble out, but the Right Reverend was nimble on his feet and around the car to catch her before she could get far. He began hauling her towards the parapet, with Franny screaming at the top of her voice and no one around to hear her.

'You can fly to God, you sinner. God awaits you, ready to take away all your wickedness. Then you will be clean and whole once more.'

Franny cried and fought for dear life, clinging tightly to the parapet as the Right Reverend first tried to push her over the side, then prise her fingers off the wall. Scarr flew at him, punching him, but it was like he was punching air. 'Help her! Help her, please,' he called to some youths who had appeared and were trying the handles of the scattered cars.

At first, they laughed, but then realized the girl's screams were in earnest and became frozen with indecision, simply staring at the Right Rev, who told them authoritatively that he was doing God's work. One of them saw the key in the Citroën and whistled to the others, who came running. The Right Reverend panicked and let go of Franny and started to his car, then realising her hadn't finished God's work turned back to the young girl. She wasn't waiting for a second chance to fly to God, but dodged around the crazy vicar and ran to the boys, who were piling into the car, dragging Franny with them.

'No, Fran! Franny, no,' Scarr shouted and flew after the car as it started away, catching hold of the door handle and running with it. He managed to open the door, but was unable to hold on as the car gathered speed and headed down the exit ramp. He turned to Rachel, who was standing alongside the man in the homburg. 'They're just as bad as this creep. Why didn't you help her? Help me stop them?'

With a weary sigh and shake of her head, she said, 'I'm

beginning to think you're a bit slow on the uptake, Mr Scarr. This is Christmas Past. She couldn't hear you, and even if she could, neither I nor you could change anything here.'

'Then how did I manage to open that car door?' he wanted to know, genuinely puzzled. 'I did pull it open, didn't I?'

'Perhaps through caring enough.'

Watching the car circling down the exit ramp and disappearing, Scarr shook his head in disbelief, then started for the stairs. Suddenly he turned back and swung a punch at the Right Reverend Portland and, to both their surprise, knocked him down.

Without commenting on this, Rachel said, 'You didn't always bury your feelings. There was someone else.'

Whether it was from knocking down the clergyman, which had sapped his energy, or his cold getting the better of him, Scarr felt very weary. He wanted to get back to his apartment and finally get into bed. Rachel had no intension of letting that happen.

Ratty would be very happy in this so-called office suite, Belle thought as she sat at one of the metal desks typing a report. The walls were badly scuffed and in need of cleaning and there was a faint odour of stale bodies where the windows hadn't been opened all winter, if they did in fact open. The unpleasant smell certainly wasn't emanating from the man who was sitting across from her, idly trying on one of her gloves, the dainty fingers of which would barely go on to his thick fingers. She liked Eddie Scarr and was pleased to have his attention, but had no intention of making things too easy for him. He was quite good looking in a rugged sort of way, if a little over-weight for his height – she guessed five-eleven, maybe six foot – his sand-coloured hair was starting to thin in the front, but that didn't put her off. He was a hard worker, which she admired and could easily have led their team and wondered why he wasn't the boss.

'What about going for a drink after you get done here?' that younger version of Scarr was casually asking. He might have been disinterested, but Belle knew that wasn't the case.

Glancing up, Belle said like she wasn't very interested, 'You don't waste any time, Eddie,' and went back to typing on the computer.

'Do you have a boyfriend?'

'If I have, he didn't tell me.'

'Do you like Indian food, Belle?'

'Not especially. I don't mind it, if it's nicely prepared for me.'

'What about Chinese?'

'The food or the people?' She smiled. 'Again, it depends what's in it.'

Getting a little exasperated, he suggested, 'Italian?'

She shook her head. 'I'm on a strict diet.'

'You sound like you'll be a cheap date.'

That made Belle smile as Scarr reached to answer a phone on the next desk, and she decided she would go out with him.

The surprise for Scarr was that she insisted they went to a restaurant that she knew. It wasn't until they were settled with a drink and picked up the menus that he realized it was a vegan establishment, with an à la carte menu. Belle hadn't said anything, so halfway through the meal he said, 'Why didn't you tell me you were vegan. I know a place where they cook very nice tender young vegans. Does it count as vegan if you eat vegans?'

'Interesting that non-vegans always have to make those sort of jokes.'

'Who said I was joking?'

'You don't like the food?'

'No, it's very good. I was enjoying it, until I heard the broccoli scream when I put my fork into it.'

'I thought that was your heart, Eddie,' she said with a straight face, 'sighing with relief.'

Scarr laughed uncertainly, then smiled to retrieve the situation. 'If I had a love affair with you,' he said brashly, 'would I have to become a vegan?'

'It would depend how much you cared –' Belle told him, leaving the question unanswered. Scarr took her hand, thinking this was a score. 'About the animals you'd otherwise have eaten,' she added.

Real dedication to the cause. Scarr hadn't suspected that about her, and it made her more attractive to him, not less.

In Belle's tiny bedroom, where they had made love at a more leisurely pace than when they first came through the door of her small apartment, with barely time to get their kit off, Scarr heard his mobile phone ringing in the next room. He could almost reach through to it as the space Belle lived in was so small, but he got out of bed and pulled on her house coat, which barely covered him. In the adjacent room he searched through his scattered clothes and found his phone, at once recognising the caller.

'What have you got?' he said and listened carefully to the details he was given. He liked mobile phones. They made alerts like this so easy, opportunities to nick wretched spongers so readily accessible.

Propped up on one elbow Belle watched Scarr return to the bedroom. He was smiling, but not for the reason she imagined. She smiled, too.

'You look very pretty in pink,' she said. 'Would you like to try one of my dresses?'

'Not my scene,' he replied in earnest. 'That was one of my contacts. The toy factory – lots of claimants working for cash.'

'Well, this is their busiest time of year with Father Christmas waiting on his sleigh. Are we going to do a raid?'

With a startled look, Scarr said, 'Are you kidding me? Are we going to raid them.' It wasn't a question.

Chapter 9

THERE WERE ALMOST NO toy manufacturers in this country any more, Rachel pointed out to Scarr as they slipped in on to the factory floor unnoticed. Her client would have known this, of course, and the fact that the only way they could compete with Asian manufactures was by employing all sorts of illegals, mostly entrapped slaves at reduced rates and without paying tax, National Insurance and Employer's National Insurance contributions, along with other benefits. But Scarr was rigid in his application and wasn't prepared to cut anyone any slack, which made Rachel wonder if, after all, she was making much of a dent in the iron-cladding that he had managed to wrap around himself.

The two dozen or so workers they found at the factory were looking beaten by life and sheepish, some a little frightened and trembling as Scarr slowly examined the orders ledger. Bob Carter came through the factory from speaking with the Indian owner; Belle and other strike-force members were questioning the workers and trying to discover their identities.

'We don't need to nick them, Eddie, do we?' Bob Carter said. Although no more senior than Eddie, most of the strike force deferred to Scarr. 'We can just get what's owed the Government. Right?'

'Some of them will be claimants, some of them outright illegals who shouldn't be here, and certainly shouldn't be enslaved by traffickers,' Scarr responded flatly without looking up from the ledger. 'We're doing them a favour.'

'C'mon, Eddie. It'll soon be Christmas. The poor slobs are just doing a bit of casual work to keep body and soul together.' He appealed to Jake Marlow with a look, him being about the closest to Scarr. Jake glanced at his mentor and laughed. He knew the score.

'According to the books, some have been working here since the summer. Fine, let them do it off benefits, like most of us.'

Dismay was what Bob's body language displayed as he walked away knowing that he'd get a more sympathetic response from a billiard ball; dismay was what Scarr felt, too, at Bob Carter's laissez-faire attitude towards this wrongdoing. Joining them and hearing part of the conversation, Belle said, 'We could give some of them a break, Eddie. A little Christmas present.'

'What, 'you planning on joining the Salvation Army with him? I expect we can find you a tambourine.' Bob looked around sharply and shook his head. With a wink at Belle, Scarr felt he was sharing with her something beyond the joke against Bob Carter.

Without warning Rachel now whisked him away to Belle's tiny apartment, where she had gone to a lot of effort making it look pretty, imagining Eddie Scarr would appreciate it. The younger Belle was wearing her prettiest dress, a pink and white Miss Selfridge taffeta puffball affair that she had bought especially for that evening. Wearing a large apron over it, careful not to get it splashed, she was busy ferrying plates and glasses from the kitchen to put the finishing touches to what was to be a candlelit dinner. She went and fetched a bottle of fairly expensive wine from the fridge and put it in an ice bucket;

after glancing at the electric clock she lit the candles, anticipating her guest, straightened the napkins and reset the cutlery, checked herself in the mirror, quickly removed her apron and fluffed out her mini dress, then did it again as nerves got the better of her.

'Do you notice anything different about Belle, Mr Scarr?' Rachel asked, hoping he was observant enough to see she was showing slightly pregnant.

'Well, she's cleaned up nicely. Then she always was a bit of a dresser – not the greatest looker, but smart, for sure.'

Rachel felt distinctly disappointed and knew just how Belle must have felt.

Smoothing her dress yet again, Belle looked at the phone as it rang, slightly startling her, then was almost afraid to answer it. Snatching it up, she blurted out, 'Where are you?' and was surprised to hear Bob Carter's voice.

'We're having an impromptu party, Belle. Come and join us, why don't you?'

'Thanks, Bob, but I'm expecting Eddie for dinner –'

'Well, good luck with that. Don't be on your own. Bring him as well – I don't suppose he's ever been to a party in his entire life!'

'I'm sure he has,' she said slightly defensively. 'We'll see.' She hung up and thought about calling Eddie, but resisted, not wanting to appear a nag or overkeen.

As she waited and waited, her party spirit gradually drained away with no word of her expected guest, even her pretty dress seemed to have deflated. She flicked through yet another magazine, then checked the time again. He was now over an hour late. Was he coming? Had he forgotten? There was no message on her phone; she had checked several times. She tossed the magazine aside, willing herself not to cry. Time crept on and finally she went to the kitchen and turned off the oven. Returning to her sitting room, Belle blew out the guttering candles. After another long wait she went to the kitchen and snapped open the rubbish bin and junked the dinner which she had so carefully prepared, then dropped the plates into the sink before bursting into tears. After a moment she resolutely shut off her tears and stiffened, determined not to feel sorry for herself.

Puzzled by this sudden change in Belle, Scarr glanced round at Rachel for an explanation. She gave him a withering look which made him so uncomfortable that he lowered his eyes.

'Like you, Belle learnt to hide her feelings to avoid being hurt.' Pointing at something beyond him, she turned his attention to another scene.

It was Bob Carter's house full of people, light and music. Children were charging through having as good a time as the adults, if drinking less alcohol. Bob grabbed Belle as she came through the door on her own and put his arm around her shoulder.

'You're far too good and kind for him, Belle.' He was a little drunk.

She removed his arm and said, 'I need a drink, Bob, not a lecture,' and headed off to where she sensed the make-shift bar was.

A little later Belle was sitting at the foot of the stairs on her own, as if her association with Scarr had contaminated her, but not for Bob Carter, who brought her a plate of food. Belle looked at it like she wasn't sure what it was, having had a little too much to drink on an empty stomach.

'It is vegan,' he said. 'You're a good influence on people. Even my kids have taken up the cause. That's a dead animal, they scream, when I mention I'd like a nice bacon sandwich."

Accepting the plate, Belle smiled and ate ravenously.

Bob Carter watched her for a moment, then said, 'You make too many excuses for him.'

'You just don't like him, Bob.'

'Do you know anyone who does – apart from you? And maybe that's changed tonight.'

'What about Jake? He does.'

That elicited a shake of his head from Bob Carter. 'All Scarr's done is make him a mirror image of himself. I don't even think those two like each other, or themselves.'

'He can be really kind at times, and funny.'

'Scarr or Jake? I refuse to believe that of either one.'

'He's the best compliance officer ever – Scarr,' Belle said in his defence.

'That doesn't commend him to the human race, Belle. He shouldn't be on the bricks anymore. Now the boss is retiring Scarr should be running the department. But I'm afraid he can't keep away from the street. He wants to be as close as he can get to the misery he causes people.'

'We don't cause them misery,' she argued. 'People do that for themselves.'

'If you take my advice, Belle, you'll give him up and get yourself a real boyfriend. One who'll support you and the baby – when it arrives.'

'How –? You must've been talking to my mum!' She caught her breath and took a long drink from her wine glass to disguise her sob.

Scarr felt chastened for the first time that he could remember. He looked round to Rachel to see if she registered this, but she wasn't there. Instead, he found her outside the strike force's offices, watching his younger self exit the building and head towards the waiting van. Belle came hurrying out after him and caught his arm, pulling him back on to the pavement. She was a little nervous and glanced over at those waiting in the van, but they seemed to have no interest in this conversation.

'Eddie – I thought I was going to see you over the holiday. We were going to have dinner, remember?'

'Oh, yes,' he said, half turning away, impatient to get going. 'Something came up. Sorry.'

'I need to talk to you about something –'

'Not a good time, Belle. We got a hot tip from an informant. We need to get going and follow it up.' He started away to the van, but then changed his mind and turned back to her. 'What did you need to say?'

Now Belle felt like her insides were turning to jelly. This wasn't how she wanted to tell him about the baby: she wasn't sure that she wanted to tell him at all now as his electric-blue eyes were flat, telling her he wasn't there. 'Oh, it's not important. It's just . . . Eddie, how would you feel . . . ?' she began, but then courage deserted her and she shook her head. After another anxious moment, she said, 'I've been invited to join a multi-agency taskforce. It means a transfer away.'

Deliberating for a moment to consider his options, Scarr said, 'When?'

'I don't have to go, Eddie. Not if you don't want me to.'

This put Scarr on the horns of a dilemma and he waited, avoiding her look as he tried to decide. Belle waited too, hopefully. They were both on the edge of something life-changing, but neither of them could quite get there. Easier for Belle as she knew what it was that she wanted, a father for the child she was expecting. She held her breath.

'No, it's the smart career move for you,' he told her, then added harshly in order to hide what he was really feeling, 'You're not much good on the street anyway, Belle. Too soft.'

Belle closed her eyes against her tears and turned away quickly, hearing the van door slam and the vehicle start away. The sting was short lived and she braced herself against the rebuff, then went resolutely into the building and didn't look back.

Now without any hesitation, Scarr stepped into the office building after Belle as if believing he could change this situation. Rachel darted in front of him, stopping him.

'That was the last you saw of her, Mr Scarr.'

'No, she came back a couple of years later to run the show – as the boss.'

'She had requested that,' Rachel informed him. This was a surprise to Scarr.

'She did? She had the baby and was a good mother by all accounts.'

Rachel inclined her head like she was acknowledging the point. 'No regrets?'

A long moment of reflection left Scarr confused and wondering what might have been. Then he moved on. 'Is there ever any point regretting what you didn't do?' He shrugged his indifference. 'Belle made her bed; I made mine. No, not really, regrets are just a waste of time. She learned to be hard. That was good for her . . . Perhaps if I'd . . . I was . . . ' More resolutely, 'No, it was for the best. Of course it was.'

Not having noticed Rachel move away, he turned only to find she was no longer with him. He searched around for her and went into the street, but couldn't see her.

'Look, stop playing games. Where are you? Where?' He ran one way, then another, panicking slightly, sensing he was missing a chance here, anxiety increasing all the while. 'Look, get me out of this nightmare. Can you hear me? Can you. I promise not to bust you. I promise – oh, no, I did that already. Look, I'm sorry. I just want this to end.'

People passed him in the street, not noticing him or his rising panic as he turned and turned again in despair.

Chapter 10

PANIC REACHED A CRESCENDO when Scarr found himself actually in the computer hammering on the inside of the screen, trying desperately to get out. What sort of material was this made of that it was so tough? He imagined computer screens were fragile things and broke easily with one whack. There was nothing hard in his possession to hit it with. Now he was certain he was going to die. Death from suffocation inside a computer; then he realized he couldn't breathe. This only increased his anxiety, if that were possible. All at once believing himself to be on the point of expiring, he suddenly burst through the screen like it was paper and tumbled over the table to land in a heap on the floor, sucking in great gulps of air. Shuffling away crab-like in case the computer pulled him in again, he stopped and looked about his room feeling foolish. He massaged his face as his breath began to normalize.

'God, what is happening to me?' Glancing around, fearing someone might answer him – anything could happen and probably would – he jumped up and ran to the mirror, but was then afraid to look into it, terrified in case he saw his younger self there. When finally he did look, it was the current hollow-cheeked, unshaven Scarr reflected back at him. Next, he spun round imagining someone was standing behind him. Who? he couldn't guess, and remained firmly convinced that he was going mad. What else could this be? Then the sound of someone groaning reached his ears, a low eerie gurgling noise like an emphysemiac which he thought was coming from the kitchen, but was too scared to venture there to investigate. He heard the groaning again and, failing to realize it was coming from himself, he said, 'I've had enough. I can't take any-more.'

Darting along the hallway past the unlit kitchen, his hands scrabbled at the locks on the door, cursing himself for having so many, none of which kept him safe. Eventually getting them all unfastened, he fled out into the night, with no idea where he was going.

Belle stopped on the church steps and turned, wearing her pretty pink and white puffball party dress and glowing like she wasn't quite real. She smiled reassuringly when she saw Eddie Scarr hurtling along the street like a startled hare that was on fire. Reaching out, she caught his arm and swung him around, stopping him. He looked at her without any immediate recognition.

'Eddie. What on earth is wrong? Where's the fire?' The reassuring smile didn't leave her face.

'Belle?' He shrank back from her, a man uncertain of any-thing. 'Is that really you?' He stared at her for a long moment and pulled back further when she reached out and touched his face. 'Is this real? Are you real, Belle? You look, well, you . . . You're so beautiful.'

Laughter erupted from Belle. 'Is *that* real – Eddie Scarr paying someone a compliment? Unreal!'

'Oh Belle, am I pleased to see you. I should have paid you a lot of compliments . . . You deserve a lot, lot more,' he said, feeling hugely relieved.

Stepping in closer to him and lacing her arm through his,

she put her hand to his forehead to feel his temperature. 'Are you all right? You're a bit warm.'

'No, I need a late-night chemist shop. I keep hallucinating. It's this cold, it's sending me mad.'

'I don't think so, Eddie,' she told him in a soothing voice. 'Come on, you have to come with me now, into the future.'

That reignited his panic and he tried to pull away from her, but found he couldn't. And curiously a part of him wanted to hold tight to her and never let go. Despite this, he said, 'Oh no, Belle, you're not in on this nonsense, are you? Give me a break, please. I've got a really heavy day tomorrow.'

'We all do, Eddie – parents up and down the country. It's Christmas Day.'

'Not that. I'm going to nail Bob Carter with the truth.'

'Good. Finally. Well, let's go inside and see him now, he's here at the Midnight Mass.'

'I can't, I have to get to a chemist's shop,' he insisted, yet allowed himself to be led without resistance of any kind up the steps into the church.

There he stood with Belle amidst the large congregation attending the mass and singing as they bathed in the warm candlelit atmosphere, no one noticing they weren't singing or even noticing their presence.

A sour note emerged from Scarr as he said, 'People are all the same: coming to church at Christmas and praying; what for? A nice few quid probably, then they go on lying and scamming the rest of the year.'

'Not everyone is like that,' Belle told him.

At this Scarr scoffed cynically. 'No? Did any single one of

this lot ever once pray without asking something for themselves?'

'You might be surprised, Eddie,' she said patiently.

Again Scarr scoffed, with a contemptuous laugh this time. 'You always were a bit gullible, Belle.'

Scarr was now beginning to try her patience, but instead of getting irritated with him, she took his hand and led him through the congregation towards the altar. Here the priest was speaking directly to the people. 'Anyone in need of special prayers for someone, perhaps someone in need of healing, please come forward.'

There was no response from anyone in the congregation as the priest waited, people looking round to their neighbour, unsure what to do. Scarr smiled smugly. He knew human nature. 'No one?' the priest asked.

Finally an old man stepped hesitantly forward.

'Since Covid, my wife developed a heart problem, then Alzheimer's, then Parkinson's.' He was clearly puzzled and upset, and explained how she had had all her vaccinations.

After encouraging people to pray for this man's wife, a middle-aged woman stepped up to the priest and said, 'My neighbour's daughter was born with a hole in her heart and has to undergo major surgery again. Can we pray for the surgeons to be successful?'

With a glance at Belle, expecting her to say, 'I told you so,' he was surprised instead to see her with tears in her eyes. Then when he turned back to the priest, he saw Bob Carter alongside of him, holding his ailing son, Tim. Resisting the urge to run forward and grab the renegade, Scarr found himself transfixed as the priest reached out and put his hands on Tim, then most bizarrely found himself urging for the boy to be healed. That caused him to bring himself up sharply. 'This is all bollocks,' he told Belle.

She put up her hand to quiet him as the priest started to speak.

'Jesus said only the halt and lame can come to the supper,' he told them. 'There he healed the sick and needy. We are all made in God's image and all of us have this gift of healing, if only we truly open our hearts. So why don't we all join hands for this special little boy, Tim, and take him into our hearts with our healing embrace?'

There was silence in the church and none of the congregation made any move to reach out to either Tim or his or her immediate neighbour, but looked around a little self-consciously to see who would start the dance. What a disappointment, Scarr was thinking. People couldn't even do this for a sick child; after all, he had nothing against this boy, only his father.

'Concentrate not on Tim's infirmity,' the priest was saying, 'but on his health. See this young man running and playing football with other children; hear his cheerful laughter and the laughter of his parents ringing out in thanks to heaven.'

Haltingly, a few members of the congregation began to reach out to their neighbours, then more joined in and those nearest to Tim started reaching out to him. Soon everyone present was clasping someone's hand, all interconnected, their eyes closed, letting their imaginations work. As he waited Scarr noticed Belle take her neighbour's hand. She glanced at him, then stretched her hand out for his. Reluctantly he took it, but couldn't break from her look that was encouraging him to go further and take his neighbour's hand. This was ridiculous. How could he do that, accepting that these people couldn't see either him or Belle? But with even greater reluctance he grasped the hand of the man next to him, surprising himself. And an even greater surprise was to follow: he could feel the man's hand, feeling some sort of energy coming through it, with the man turning and smiling at him like he was a physical presence and could see him.

No, this was complete nonsense, Scarr told himself. He wasn't feeling anything, but imagining it all and let go of the imagined hand. He turned to Belle as the congregation began to disperse. 'What good will that do him or any of these other fools?' he said.

Without replying Belle turned to the Carter family who were heading towards the exit, Tim asleep in Bob Carter's arms, Kim affectionately brushing hair off her son's face. People were reaching out and touching Tim as they passed and wishing the family well. One eccentric old lady came up to them and touched Tim's face with her gnarled, arthritic fingers. At once she grabbed Scarr's attention.

'I know her –'

'Bring Tim to this address tomorrow,' Mrs Thompson said with a quiet authoritative voice that somehow you couldn't dismiss. Scarr was surprised, he had never heard his neighbour speak before, other than in frightened grunts as she hurried away from him. 'Be sure to bring him, won't you.' She gave Bob Carter a piece of paper with the address.

Scarr pressed in to read it, thinking he could maybe bust Carter there rather than in front of all his children. He had nothing against them, he reminded himself. All that was written in her spider's crawl was: Sheepcote. Sparse as it was, he would locate it all right on Google Maps. Suddenly he stiffened, aware that Belle was watching him.

'I know what your game is here!' he told her.

'I'm trying to get you to consider an alternative position about Bob.' A knowing smile fell over Belle's still pretty face and she inclined her head in the direction of the way out. Only it wasn't the way out, Scarr found as he went with her.

The phone Bob carried rang and rang unanswered, deepening Kim's worry. Again she crossed the sitting room to check through the window for her husband and youngest child's return. She didn't know how many times she'd checked, and each time only added to her anxiety. Scarr stepped back from her path as she peered out on to the snow-falling street. There were no suspicious-looking vehicles with men sitting in them waiting to grab Bob, but that of itself didn't give her any comfort. Something had happened to him and Tim, she was sure. She even thought of calling the police, but decided against it. While the two middle children were caught up with the Christmas presents they had received, Martha was at her mother's side sharing her concern.

'Where are they?' Kim said, addressing the question to herself and not expecting an answer. 'Why doesn't he answer his phone? Something's wrong. Something must have happened.'

'No, it's all right, mum. Or we'd have heard.'

'I should have taken Tim to that place instead of your dad, especially with that awful Eddie Scarr being around.'

'I don't think he's human,' Martha observed quietly. Scarr heard this and her words bit into him. Was it really what the girl thought or was she just being influenced by her parents?

He glanced at Belle, who was still with him. She had heard, too, and simply raised her eyebrows as if to say, well, you asked for it. Whether he did or didn't deserve it, the words were still wounding.

Worry caused Kim to distractedly pick up some of the toys off the floor and put them down again, then pick the same toys up and put them down once more before going out into the kitchen to check on the Christmas dinner. Then Martha picked up the same toys and hesitated as if deciding what to do with them. Finally she threw them to the floor.

'Why don't you do something useful for a change, instead of bickering all the time?' she said sharply to her siblings.

'Why don't you shut up bossing?' Dan retorted. He swiped some toys off the table defiantly. 'You're not the boss.'

Scarr waited for a response from the girl, but there was none. She turned and went out. He followed her. He wasn't done with this one, wanting to get even with her for what she said about him.

In the kitchen Martha shuffled up to the table and picked at some raw pastry. Kim looked up at her from peeling Brussel sprouts and gave her a distracted smile. 'You can roll that out, if you like, love – not too much or it'll go hard.' She liked it when the children helped her, but wouldn't demand that they did. They had plenty to cope with in their own worlds, especially with the amount of homework the school piled on them. Their dad was good about helping them. That got her worrying again, wondering what could have happened to him and Tim. What if he wasn't coming back? What if he'd been carted off to prison? Being one of nature's philosophers, she was sure her husband would probably cope with that, but she wasn't sure she and the children would.

'Why can't they help?' Martha said as she started to roll the pastry.

Lost in thought, Kim didn't reply.

After a moment, Martha said hesitantly, 'Mum, I didn't say a prayer for Tim in the church last night. I'm sorry.'

Kim turned and smiled. 'That's all right, Martha. You shoulder too much responsibility as it is, lovey. It's really not fair to you.'

'Instead, I said one for that man who's chasing dad. I prayed for him to change –'

'Eddie Scarr?' There was shock in her voice. 'Well, that's what I call real optimism! All the prayers in the world won't change his rotten cold heart.'

Hearing this change of heart from the girl made Scarr instantly reassess what he thought about her, if not change himself. She had no reason to like him or pray for him and it left him wondering, when he heard the front door bang. The two women in the kitchen turned, suddenly excited.

'It's them!' Martha exclaimed and rushed through with her mother.

Scarr was amazed that anyone like Bob Carter could have such an effect on people, even his own family. Could they be as venal as he believed Carter to be, or were they corrupted by him? Or perhaps he was wrong all this while about Carter. Was that possible? Before he got an answer, he hurried after them with Belle to see what was going on.

The hallway was too narrow for a wrestling match, but that's what it looked like as the two middle children clambered over their dad trying to claim his attention with, 'Dad. Daddy!' showing him a book or how a new toy worked as he tried to set Tim down.

'Yes, yes, my darlings, let me get in and get my coat off first –'

'How did you get on?' Kim was eager to know. 'Did you see the old lady?'

'I ran,' Tim told her excitedly. 'I ran all the way back.'

'The old woman wasn't there – did we imagine her, Kim?' Bob asked, genuinely puzzled. 'There wasn't even a house at the Sheepcote address, just some sort of garden. A gardener was there pruning roses.'

'Working on Christmas Day? He must be a relative of Scarr's.'

'He spoke to me,' Tim told them proudly. 'He said he would see me again very soon, mum.'

'What does that mean? Was he funny, like the old lady?' As she said this, she felt pressure on her heart, like someone was crushing it.

'He wasn't funny,' Tim said, offering her a white rose. 'He gave me this.'

'Oh, it's lovely, Tim.' Fear was pressing in on her now and she dared not take her eyes off the child, irrationally fearing he would suddenly disappear.

'He said it was for you, mum, so you would always remember me.'

'How could I ever forget you, my darling?' She busied herself removing his coat, fighting tears that were trying to spring from her eyes, relieved when Tim ran off to play with some toys, the other children following; then she wanted to know about the man in the garden. Bob at once caught hold of his wife and held her close with tears in his eyes, too.

'Kim . . . ' he began in a tear-choked voice. 'He wasn't a gardener. He . . . I think he was . . . ' He couldn't finish the sentence. He stiffened and tried again. 'He told Tim how he'd soon be joining him in his wonderful garden,' he managed in a quiet voice, when the dam burst and tears flooded out of him.

Watching this in frozen trepidation, Scarr realized he was holding his breath; then he realized he was also crying. That was something he had no memory of ever doing since that young boy had cried himself to sleep in the care home. He looked round to see if Belle had noticed his reaction, only she wasn't there.

Chapter 11

BUSYING HERSELF LIKE A PERSON possessed was the only way Kim could deal with her increasing stress. Keeping active was how she managed a lot of things that might otherwise have overwhelmed her in their current situation. Here she was grabbing up toys and books from the sitting room floor, along with all sorts of torn present wrappings, growing more and more irritable and shouting at Martha, who was nearest to hand. 'You shouldn't leave these on the floor to get broken. We don't have money to throw away.'

'I didn't leave them there,' Martha shouted back, giving as good as she got. Scarr could see that she was stressed, too. This young woman was suffering and he felt a bit sorry for her. But knew it was her father who had brought this down on her and the rest of the family. The wretched man should just do the right thing.

'Help pick them up and don't argue with me –'

'Don't pick on me. It's not fair –'

'Well what is fair, d'you think? Me doing everything?'

'It's always me, it's always me,' the girl screamed and started to run.

Bob Carter put his arm out and caught her then gave her a squeeze, before collecting things off the floor. 'Come on, let's not pick on anyone. Not today,' he said. 'We'll make it a special Christmas Day for Tim.'

'You spoil them –'

'Kim,' he responded calmly. It was clear to Scarr that he

knew it was all his fault and was treading on eggshells around his family, his wife especially.

That was the last straw for Kim. She slammed into him with, 'You're never here nowadays to deal with these problems. I can't take all the moving around, frightened even to open the door.'

With that she ran out and along to the kitchen, slamming the door. Then there was silence and Bob and the children waited, expecting something else to follow. When it didn't, they gave each other uncertain looks. In silence and all together they began to gather the debris and any presents which had been left on the floor. It was Ella who broke the silence.

'Dad, can you stay with us all the time now?' she asked. 'Can you?'

''Course he can't,' Martha snapped.

That caused the atmosphere to become fragile again as Bob looked round at each of the four earnest, expectant faces. Breathless now, Scarr waited to see if he'd answer. Wishing.

Finally Bob nodded his assent before closing his eyes with hopeful reassurance. Was this it then? Scarr wondered, but felt no sort of elation as he turned to Belle to check her reaction, only again she had disappeared.

She hadn't gone far, only to the Carter's kitchen where Kim was frantically scrubbing at a saucepan like she couldn't get it clean enough. Bob Carter stepped in and put his arms around her from behind. After a few moments she stopped scrubbing and threw the scourer back into the water and tensed. Her husband started to gently massage her shoulders.

'I'm afraid for Timmy, Bob,' Kim said rationally. 'That man

in the garden, I don't like what he said. I mean, who was he?'

'I don't know. But Tim seemed to like him. He was very happy about walking around the garden with him holding his hand.'

'I'm frightened for him.' She turned in his arms, her face a mosaic of worries. 'And for you. He'll come for you – Scarr. You know he will.'

Bob kissed her gingerly, unsure of the reception he'd get, and when she responded, he went further and said, 'I'm not running anymore. I've got nothing to hide or be ashamed of. I was working undercover for Jake Marlow. I'll eventually prove it, you see.'

This should've been music to Scarr's ears, only it wasn't. Without enthusiasm he managed to clap his hands together and he even hugged and kissed Belle in an attempt to show his excitement. But his words 'Brilliant, Belle, brilliant. Now we'll grab him easily,' were flat and a bit listless. Then turning, he saw Bob Carter kiss his wife passionately like he had not a worry in the world, 'Merry Christmas!' he was saying while the four children crowded in the doorway smirking and giggling, not having seen their parents this way in a long while. 'Yeah, one big happy family,' Scarr managed to say, '– until the hammer falls,' But felt mean saying it.

Next Belle took him to the sitting room where the whole family was around the table. This was strewn with the remnants of their Christmas dinner, a half-finished pudding with a piece of holly on it, wine and cans of Coke; cherries were being eaten and Christmas crackers pulled. Children merrily flicked the cherry stones at one another, and unfurled paper hats and checked out the novelties and jokes from the crackers. Ella put a hat on her father, then put her arms affectionately around his neck, giving Eddie Scarr pause; even Kim was smiling, content with her family at this moment. Martha unfurled a joke and read it aloud.

'What do you call a dog who answers the telephone?' The younger children remained silent. 'A golden receiver –!'

Suddenly without warning, Tim went into spasm, unable to get any breath at all into his lungs and very soon began to turn purple. Kim saw him first and screamed, 'Tim!' as Bob dived across the table to him. This was her worst nightmare; the strange man in the garden instantly coming into her mind inviting Tim to join him soon. This was it. Tim dying and none of them being able to prevent it.

'He can't breathe,' Bob said, holding Tim, who was struggling as panic caught fire around him, 'Calm down everyone. C'mon, Tim, get your breath. You can do it. C'mon on, my lovely boy, breathe, Timmy. Please boy –'

'Oh Dear God, dear God. Do something, Bob –' Kim entreated.

'I'm trying, I'm trying,' Bob responded as panic tried to get a foothold.

None of the children were calming as instructed but were in a rising uproar, calling Timmy's name as if their voices alone would save him.

'Where's his puffer? Where is it? Get it –'

Since his return earlier Tim had been doing so well that his medication was completely forgotten. Now Dan came running with it and Bob put it in the boy's mouth, urging him to breathe, but to no avail. Tim was turning a deeper shade of purple. Mother was crying and beseeching God to help; dad was urging; the other children were screaming and crying as Scarr stepped among them, seeing at once what the problem was.

'His windpipe is blocked,' he announced authoritatively. 'What are you, dim? There's a cherry stone stuck in his windpipe. Can't you see what the problem is?' No one responded, of course. 'Get out the way – this is what you do –'

As the family continued to panic, Scarr stepped in behind Tim and, reaching his arms around him from behind, locked his fists over his tiny diaphragm and gave an upwards thump, having been taught the Heimlich manoeuvre on a First Aid course he had attended. Nothing happened, so he tried again. Again nothing happened to help Tim, who was now turning a deep shade of blue as death claimed him. Finally, Scarr turned to Belle and pleaded earnestly, 'Help me, Belle! I can't do it.'

Belle was the only calm person in the room. 'You certainly can,' she replied.

Next Scarr turned and tried to seize hold of Bob, but could get neither his attention nor any purchase on his body, his arms were simply passing through him. 'For pity's sake, man, there's a cherry stone stuck in his windpipe,' he screamed in his face. 'Put your arms around his little diaphragm and pull sharply upwards. Do it now before it's too late.'

With quiet amusement Belle watched Scarr's rising desperation, impressed by his concern, thinking how there was hope for him yet as a member of the human race.

The sound now filling the room was Kim's screaming at

her son's demise, blotting out all logical and reasoned thinking. Stepping out of his frail body, Tim went and joined Belle, taking her hand as if expecting to be led away.

'Am I going to see the nice man in the garden now?' he asked.

Turning sharply at the boy's voice, Scarr saw him start away with Belle, and knowing at once what that meant, he gave a brutal cry, 'No!' Then using all his natural and supernatural force he finally managed to push Bob's hands around Tim's tiny body and helped him make the upward thump of the Heimlich manoeuvre, causing the cherry stone to shoot out of Tim's mouth. To Scarr's great relief, and that of everyone else in the room, the boy desperately sucked in air, as much and as fast as he could, while his shadow-self let go of Belle's hand and slipped back into his physical body. Everyone cried with relief and touched him and hugged him and patted him and kissed him.

Getting control of himself and the situation, Bob Carter said, 'Let him breathe, let him have some air. Breathe, Tim. Big slow breaths like we taught you.' He breathed deeply and slowly with Tim. 'God, son, you really gave us a big scare just then.'

Belle watched Scarr as he observed this happy family reunion with some pleasure, a smile creasing his cheeks. Then suddenly aware of Belle watching him, he appeared caught out and his smile vanished.

Bob gave his youngest son a sip of water as he recovered, then his wife almost smothered him with hugs and kisses in her relief. 'Oh, Timmy, my darling, you had us so worried. You really did.'

'Why?' Tim asked, puzzled. 'What's wrong?'

'You almost died, you twat,' Ella piped up.

'But that man just there helped me.' He turned and looked directly at Scarr, pointing to him. Bob turned with the whole family, looking in the direction of Scarr and Belle, but not seeing anything.

'What man just where, Tim?'

'Can he see me, Belle?' Scarr whispered in case he was being heard.

'He knows you, dad,' Tim explained. 'It was him who made you thump me here,' – indicating his diaphragm.

With a nervous laugh, Bob Carter said, 'What? Well, someone was certainly helping us, that's for sure.'

'Oh Bob,' Kim said, gripping his arm, 'I've gone all shivery. It must have been the man in the garden.'

That caused Bob to turn back to the empty space where Scarr and Belle were standing, shaking his head, confused.

'Does Tim die?' Scarr asked, and pressed the point when Belle didn't immediately answer him. 'Does he?'

Belle scoffed. 'I can't see why it matters to you. He's not your child.'

Brought up short by his unsettled feelings, Scarr said in an uncertain fashion, 'No, well, I mean . . . It wasn't him who killed Jake, it was Bob, well in all probability.'

'So you keep saying.' Belle was now growing impatient. 'After his dad goes to prison Tim suffers a massive seizure –'

'But does he die? I need to know. I mean, I just helped to save him.'

'Huh, d'you want a medal? What value are people like Tim

Carter? Useless feeders! That's what you called his kind, Eddie.'

Crestfallen, Scarr lowered his head and mumbled, 'It's my job, Belle, it robs you of humanity. But someone has to stay on top of these people.'

No ground did Belle give, she simply said, 'Then you know the answer, know exactly where you're driving this.' With that she stormed out, showing her disappointment. Scarr flew after her.

'It's his dad's fault,' he argued, trying to justify his position. 'If Carter hadn't gone bent, Jake and me wouldn't have been lured into a trap with that wretched human trafficker. End of story.'

If looks could kill Scarr would've been dead when Belle turned and gave him a look that could have peeled the skin off a crocodile. He jumped back from her, but wasn't done with this.

'Jake got stabbed! Remember?'

'You think I could forget, Eddie? He was one of my team.' She paused and considered him for a long moment, making him feel more uncomfortable. 'Maybe we could break the rules here and take a closer look at just what happened back then.'

'Don't we know what happened?' Scarr said angrily, trying to push away any doubt as he remembered the events surrounding Jake's death.

'Do we really?' Belle asked evenly now. 'Are you sure you're not simply blinded by your own need to blame someone for your own shortcomings?' She nodded him away.

Why was he going along with all this nonsense? Not just going back to see Jake being killed and by whom, but all this cold-filled rubbish about past and future events. Why couldn't he just wake up and find himself free of this nightmare and getting ready to go and collar Bob Carter?

That wasn't happening. Instead, he was dragged along to a familiar isolated warehouse late at night, watching with Belle as the headlights from a white van bounced across the rubble-strewn yard and the van came to a stop. With about as much grace as three deflating lorry-tyre inner tubes, Aram Guli oozed out followed by Bob Carter.

'We only take them what's fully paid up what's owing,' Guli said. 'Got that clear, son?' He glanced about cautiously, then unlocked the wicket-gate within the big roller shutter door. Glancing about again before he squeezed inside with Bob.

Here soiled mattresses were placed about the floor space, some with make-shift curtains rigged up to afford a meagre sort of privacy; empty tin cans were spilling from a rubbish sack and a dozen or so illegal immigrants looking in not very good shape were watching the new arrivals expectantly. Among them was the stick-thin, worried looking Ethiopian mother, Mrs Achebe with her three children. She edged forward hopefully from her sleeping area as Guli waddled past and tapped four men from different ethnic groups on the shoulder like they were being given an award. In a sense they were.

'S'your lucky day, boys,' he said cheerfully. 'Your sponsors paid up, so you got a room and work to go to.'

'Me, sir,' Mrs Achebe said pressing forward, 'I work very hard. Hard work I can do, sir. Yes, please.'

A cynical laugh rattled Guli's four chins. 'Sure you can, lady – when your relatives come up with the balance of what's owed on you. They'd better come up with it soon. I'm not a charity.'

'No, sir,' Mrs Achebe insisted, 'I work, I pay, sir.'

'What, you think I'm stupid? It was you what came off the boat, lady, not me! Press them relatives of yours harder for my money.'

As Guli moved away, Bob Carter gave the Ethiopian woman a friendly wink then caught up with the boss who started to squeeze back through the narrow wicket gate with the 'award-winners'. 'If she can sew, Aram, the sweatshop could use her. They're desperate for machinists. You could put a lien on whatever wages they pay her. What about it?'

Three inner-tubes Guli was dubious, but saw the logic in this and not having to provide food for these people. He eased his great bulk back out of the small aperture, then addressed Mrs Achebe. 'Can you work a sewing machine, dear?'

'Yes, sir. Very fast worker, sir,' came the urgent reply.

With a final nod, Guli motioned to Bob Carter to bring her with the others. 'At least we won't have to go on feeding her hungry mob.'

Scarr was growing increasing frustrated. This was a big waste of time as far as he was concerned. 'It doesn't bring Jake back,' he said, 'but it does nail Carter for the rat he is.'

'No. It doesn't change the narrative at all,' Belle argued. 'Your problem with Bob wasn't any possible guilt, but his humanity. You couldn't live with that. Jake was just as bad.'

'Humanity? Blokes like that should be in the Salvation Army, not on the strike force. I know what I know, Belle, and you've just proved it.'

'You're so absolute, Eddie, you only see things in black and white. Sometimes it helps to blur the lines with a little grey to avoid a bigger disaster.'

'Whatever happens to these people they bring it on themselves.'

'Let me show you the result of one of your black and white decisions.'

'Forget it. I need to go home to bed –'

Before he could protest further, she yanked him away to a detention centre that had a peculiar smell to it, one he'd never noticed before and was unsure if it was real. The smell was depression, he decided. It was so strong you could almost bottle it. Illegal immigrants sat around in this dingy building with nothing to occupy themselves; all nationalities having little or no means of communication in their fear and confusion, and nothing to distract them other than an explosion of unprovoked hostility at some minor infraction by a fellow detainee and the constant drone of television which most couldn't understand. None of them bore any relation to Scarr, as far as he knew, so he didn't understand why he had been brought here.

'They're all illegals,' he said, but Belle wasn't listening as she moved through them on to a corridor, dragging him with her. 'They have to be sent back to where they came from. How many of these people do you think our tiny island can go on supporting?'

Still Belle made no attempt to answer, but opened a door on a corridor with Scarr at her heels. There on the edge of a narrow wooden bunk bed that had seen a lot of wear was Mrs Achebe with her three young children. She was reading to them from a *Ladybird Key Words* book.

'Peter-can-write. Jane-can-write –' She suddenly looked up in alarm as the door opened without anyone knocking. The detention centre superintendent entered uninvited with two social workers and instinctively Mrs Achebe drew her children closer to herself for protection.

'We don't have enough staff to safeguard your children here,' the superintendent announced. 'Not with all these men here. The kids have to go with these ladies, Mrs Achebe.'

Mrs Achebe had enough English to understand what was being told her. 'Oh no, sir,' she protested, 'they must not leave me. I look after.'

Brooking no discussion, the beefy superintendent reached out for the children as the two social workers closed in, making the tiny room very crowded. 'C'mon now, let's be sensible about this, dear –'

The first social worker, who looked as though her stick-thin colleague could fit inside her, tried to separate the children from their mother, causing pandemonium. Mrs Achebe gripped them harder and the frightened children clung to mother tighter as their distress became deeper and more vocal.

'Mrs Achebe lost three of her other children back in Ethiopia –' Belle explained, hoping to move Scarr.

'Then she should have stayed there and tried to find them,' he snapped defensively, not wanting to get drawn into this.

'You really don't mean that, Eddie, do you?' Belle said, a little disappointed as she tried to meet his look. He wouldn't look at her and wished he hadn't replied as he had. 'Life was pretty tough for her back home. Very few people living in this country would have survived it. She managed to scrape up the money to pay traffickers to bring them here, but then the operation this end upped the price.'

'Come on, Belle,' Scarr said wearily, still not meeting her eyes, 'you've been in this game long enough. Everyone gives you their lump-in-the-throat story. I've heard it all before and I'm sick of it. First, we let it go for her, then someone else, then another lot and soon we're overrun with them.'

That made Belle wonder if this man was worth going on with any further, finding his attitude was crushing her heart. But she had come this far now, so decided to try a little harder.

The social workers finally separated the children from their mother and steered them out into the corridor, but they weren't going quietly. With all the screaming and the ensuing chaos, Mrs Achebe suddenly grabbed hold of all three children and raced them away along the narrow corridor. She dived into the kitchen just as someone emerged, here she slammed the door after herself and wedged a sturdy stool hard under the handle.

With a heavy sigh the superintendent said, 'Oh dear, I can see this getting difficult. I'll call the local police to get them out.' He pulled a phone from his pocket as the social workers hammered and shoved on the unyielding kitchen door to reason with this stupid woman – according to their way of thinking. Neither had children of their own.

In the not-very-clean, grey painted kitchen, Belle and her reluctant companion watched as Mrs Achebe clutched her kids close to herself, ignoring the hammering on the door and the two women beseeching her to let the children out. Her gaze slowly circled the room with its two large gas stoves, the double sink, the table with knives lined up against the chopping board, the windows with their safety locks which would allow them to only open so far, and the padlocked larder door. Finally her gaze came back to settle on the lined-up carving knives and didn't move from them.

'No, don't even think about it, lady,' Scarr told her with some concern. 'That'll just bring more heartache, love.' He turned to Belle.

She simply shrugged, as if it was of no consequence to her. 'It would solve a lot of problems for us and the country, Eddie.'

'Not really. Come on, I don't like the way this situation is shaping up.'

They watched the mother sit her youngest child down on the work surface and go to the windows. She reached through the bars and closed each of the small apertures, then dropped the dusty Venetian blinds. Next, she opened both oven doors and turned on the gas taps. Gathering her children, she brought them over to the ovens and settled on the floor with them, cuddling them close to her and ignoring the banging on the door. Now Scarr gave Belle an urgent look, like he was waiting for her to do something to stop this, but she didn't respond.

'Belle,' he appealed anxiously, 'you gotta stop her – having your kids taken away is just not worth this.'

At first the appeal fell on deaf ears and brought forth no action. Then an argument. 'How would you know what it means for a mother to lose her children?'

'Well, at least they'll have a roof over their heads,' he said lamely, 'and a bed and regular food.' When still no action from Belle transpired, he raced across the room and tried to turn off the gas taps, only he couldn't move them.

'Soon we'll be overrun with these people,' Belle said provocatively.

The look he gave her startled Belle and once more she began to think perhaps there was hope for him after all.

'This isn't the answer.'

With a sharp tone of voice, Belle said, 'Eddie, stop being so damned inconsistent. This woman and her kids are just the tip of the iceberg, you said it often enough. You're right, of course.'

'No, we have to try to find an answer in their country of origin, That's the way to stop them coming here illegally and putting themselves at risk.'

'You can't right the whole world. You have to deal with what is now, and these illegals are a big problem –' still being provocative.

Anger flared in Scarr, threatening to blow all his brain cells. Never in all his life had he felt more ineffectual than at that moment. He turned in frustration to Mrs Achebe and shouted at her to turn off the gas, expecting her to hear him and be able to respond. The only reaction from the woman was to pull her children even closer to herself and kiss each in turn and generally fuss with them, making them more comfortable in their last moments here on earth.

'It's no use,' Belle reminded him, 'they can't hear you.'

'Then you help them. Don't stand by and watch them go like this. Belle?' There was no response from her. 'Okay, look, I could be wrong. Maybe I am wrong about her. She could be genuine.'

Quietly Belle smiled and opened a folder she had with her. 'No, you're quite right, Eddie. Look, she came here in a container lorry from France with her children, and no means of support.'

'No, she was working hard in that sweatshop we busted – perhaps we shouldn't have done,' he said growing more and more anxious as he waited for Belle to meet him on this. Only she didn't budge. 'Where's that detention centre superintendent? Get him to break down the door. These unhelpful people are never around when you need them.'

He tried to open a window, but his hand simply passed through the lever. Next, he turned to the stoves and tried again to shut off the gas, getting more distressed when the taps wouldn't budge no matter how hard he tried to move them. Grabbing Belle to help him only seemed to make the gas hiss louder, he could now see it filling the room. 'Please, Belle, help her.' His plea was from the bottom of his heart. 'Why won't you help them? Has this job made you lose all your compassion?'

'Hah, that's rich, coming from you,' she said. 'I can't help them, any more than you can. Anyway, my time here is now running out –'

This caused an entirely different anxiety to rise like acid bile in Scarr's mouth and almost choke him. 'What?' he said in panic as if he hadn't heard her. 'You're not . . . ? Nothing's going to happen to you, Belle, is it?' The possibility was scrambling his mind. What was the answer that was staring him in the face? The future! Yes, this was the future, he could somehow stop this happening, but how? Panic didn't subside in him when he heard the Achebes starting to choke.

Finally he got to it. 'Okay, I was wrong here. Who could blame this mother for wanting a better life –?' The fading Mrs

Achebe turned and looked in his direction as if having heard what he said. It was like she saw Scarr in faint outline as he reached out to help her up off the floor, then his hand guided hers on to the gas taps and one by one shut them off. Now he helped her reach over and raise the blind before opening some windows, when the door crashed in, knocking the stool over. A young policewoman rushed in with an even younger and shorter policeman, followed by the unit superintendent and the two social workers. They helped Mrs Achebe scoop up her children and shepherd them out into the corridor. Scarr helped her pick up a child's soft toy as the policeman reached through the bars and opened more windows.

'Someone help this poor family,' Scarr said, looking at the superintendent.

'Perhaps she needs a psychiatric referral,' he responded as he steadied Mrs Achebe and reached out his phone.

Quickly Scarr stepped in close to the policewoman and said, 'No. You're supposed to light the gas when you're making pizza, love.'

Pricking up her ears as if in reaction to this, the young policewoman repeated his words verbatim, and stayed the superintendent's hand, preventing him punching the numbers on his phone. 'You won't find a place for her today,' she said.

Pleased with what he could seemingly achieve, he stepped nearer to the stick-thin social worker and whispered to her, causing her to turn in his direction as if she was seeing and hearing Scarr. She repeated his words. 'No. Let's find them a placement together . . . What? Did I just say . . . ?' She shook her head as if unsure what she had just said. 'Yes, that's best. It won't be easy, but we'll try.'

Satisfied, Scarr turned to look for Belle as the large social worker was nodding with tears in her eyes. 'There, you see, Belle . . . Belle?'

Belle was disappearing along the corridor like Cinderella from the ball at the stroke of midnight. Running hard after her, Scarr just managed to catch hold of her dress.

'Belle, don't leave me. Belle –? I – I do love you,' he managed to say, but couldn't hold her. To his alarm the dress leaked through his hand like water and the door banged in her wake. As he tried to go after her he found he couldn't, the door was a solid wall that he was unable to pass through.

Chapter 12

THE WHARFSIDE HOUSING ESTATE he was now approaching was familiar, yet different and it took Scarr a few moments to realize it was his estate. He looked around at the place, disorientated; it had changed almost beyond recognition and he couldn't quite get his bearing. Was that so surprising after all that had happened to him? The prospect of suing the manufacturers of Benylin for the strange and disconcerting experiences it had brought him and where it had put his head was little comfort. They would probably laugh him out of court and tell him how people went to all sorts of exotic places and paid shedloads of money for the sort of experiences he had had. Perhaps he would keep quiet about that, find his apartment and his bed and put it all behind him with some solid sleep.

Looking down, he saw he had a child's soft toy in his hand, a furry elephant. Where did that come from and how the hell did he get it? Was this whole nightmare starting up again? No, he was on his way home from work, he reasoned; he had a head cold; he was going to bed to get rid of it and tomorrow organize a raid to pick up the runaway Bob Carter.

Without warning Bob Carter was at his side, smiling as if nothing was amiss in his world. 'Playing at Father Christmas again, Eddie?' he said cheerfully.

Immediately Scarr tried to hide the toy, like it was something shameful to be caught with and found himself feeling embarrassed. Then he remembered he had been wearing a Father Christmas disguise as he was watching the sweatshop prior to the raid, that's when he had seen Bob Carter. Now he was here. What was that about? The answer came at once.

'Ready to see more of your future, Eddie?'

'I'm going home. This is my apartment block – I think,' he replied, puzzled. 'What happened here?'

'Neglect. No one bothers about their neighbours. Nobody cares anymore.'

'Of course we do. People do care. What are you saying?' As if in answer to his question the black and white dog suddenly bounded up to Scarr like an old friend pleased to see him. The feeling wasn't mutual. 'Oh, it's you again. What do you want now? Didn't I just give you most of my supper?'

'He's giving you another chance, Eddie. He wants to be your friend. You're a bit short of those.'

'Friends with anyone who gives him food, more like it. Watch this – he does tricks.' He turned to the dog. 'Beg.' The dog just sat and watched him expectantly. 'Well, sometimes.'

'Did you know Mr Al Fayed in number 33?' Bob asked.

There was confusion in Scarr's expression as he tried to recall this person and when no face came with the name, he said, 'Is he newly moved in?'

'He certainly was – eight years ago. He died recently and no one even noticed. His cat was dead too when Social Services eventually found him.'

Caught out, Scarr looked round sharply at Bob Carter to see if he was joking, then past him along his walkway where three boys were larking around, making a noise. One was tall and stringy like a basket-ball player and called Elroy. Scarr felt pleased about knowing this, and that he lived with his single mum in the next block. Why he remembered these details was because she was on benefits. Elroy and his friends were teasing the old and eccentric Mrs Turner, tossing her packet of biscuits to each other out of her reach and laughing. They suddenly looked up startled by the unseen approach of Scarr and Bob. Dropping the packet, they edged around the old woman as if scared of something, then finally fled. Mrs Turner muttered something incomprehensible and stooped and picked up her biscuits; she checked around, then let herself into her apartment and locked the door.

'Do you know her name, Eddie?' Bob asked.

'What is this, a test?' Scarr replied irritably.

'Or that Mrs Turner will die of loneliness?' he continued.

Deflecting the question, Scarr said, 'Why doesn't someone call the police about those kids? They're real pests at times. Not that the police will ever do much.'

He was to get more than he bargained for.

'The police are on their way,' Bob Carter told him.

Below, a police car arrived unhurriedly and two policemen dressed as if for war climbed out and ambled towards Scarr's building as a neighbour, unknown to him, scurried out of a door on the ground floor to meet them. Soon the policemen were coming up the stairs to Scarr's landing, causing him to smile triumphantly at Bob.

'You see, some of us do care! You should get after those kids in the next block,' he said, addressing the police officers, both of whom were out of breath from climbing the stairs. Then he tried, 'Along there in the next block. The complainant, my neighbour, is Mrs Turner, she's just in there –' pointing ineffectually to where she lived. The police, as he suspected, weren't interested, nor were they interested in the trouble-makers; they went instead to Scarr's apartment. Why? Was someone making a vicious complaint against him, trying to get him into trouble? He would soon see. 'Hey, not there. That's my apartment.'

The police couldn't hear him, of course, and began hammering on the door. Bob nodded in their direction. 'Are you sure you want to see this, Eddie?'

'What are you talking about?' He edged closer to his apartment and noticed something strange. 'Why are the windows black?' Along with one of the policemen he tried to peer through the window, while the other uniform continued hammering on the door and calling his name. This brought Mrs Turner out of her apartment and along to join them. She wasn't a mumbling loon after all, he realized, but quite articulate.

'It's months since I've seen him, officer,' she said in a clear voice. 'Not a very friendly neighbour. Lonely, I'd say. No one ever visited him. First, I noticed the windows getting blacker and blacker and thought perhaps he'd put up black-out drapes to shut out the world – that's what he's like, I'm afraid. But then I noticed the awful smell emanating from there. That's when I telephoned your people to report it.'

Both policemen began kicking their heavy boots against the door. After repeated kicks the three locks began to yield.

'Do you want to go inside and see what's happened?' Bob asked, his tone not without sympathy or concern.

With frightening realisation and growing apprehension, Scarr said, 'They're flies . . . Flies, on the windows.'

Finally, the door burst open as the jamb split apart, when Scarr's groans of despair matched the shocked response of the policemen, who immediately folded back in panic as swarms of flies rushed out, along with a cloying, choking smell. The two policemen stepped away completely, sucking in some of the flies with their gulps of breath, the air now thick with them. Then Scarr saw Elroy and his gang who had come up to investigate; they were holding their noses and peering into the apartment.

'You notice how the unloved have such a peculiar smell about them, Eddie?'

As one of the cops started retching badly, the other managed to get on the radio to their base. ' . . . We can't get near the place to see if foul-play was involved. We'll need the brigade here with breathing equipment, and the public health people. Whoever it is in there, he must have been dead for weeks.'

In his sitting room Scarr watched people from the fire and public health service in heavy breathing gear and shiny white fumigation suits, spraying the apartment with insecticide to kill the remaining flies and their maggots. Others in protective clothing and respirators approached the maggot-crawled corpse. Scarr stood rooted to the ground and stared in horror at the unrecognisable, shrivelled, blackened body. Words caught in his throat as he tried to speak, and when he at last managed to make a sound, it was a hoarse croak that seemed to emanate from outside of him. He attempted to moisten his lips but found he had no saliva. The longest minute of his life passed before he somehow managed speech.

'Please tell me that's not me, Bob. Tell me it isn't – dying like this without a friend in the world.'

There was only a heavy silence from Bob Carter, with the hiss of spray guns filling the air.

'Not a single friend?' Scarr asked on the verge of tears.

'That dog was friendly enough,' Bob said. 'He was probably your only friend and you rejected him.'

A sob escaped from Scarr now as he stared at his corpse; he was on the edge of breaking down completely and muttered, 'I'm not the man I was.' Not knowing what to do, he waited. After a while he drew himself up to his full ghostly height and said defiantly, 'I will not allow myself to be the man who brought this tragedy upon himself. I will not.'

With a hollow laugh, Bob said, 'Just words, Eddie. Words alone are meaningless. Only actions can steer you away from this end.'

What actions? Now with remorse etched into his face as deep as a grave, he turned in the direction of his guide, but Bob Carter was no longer present, only the blue-tinged air where the health people continued spraying their noxious fumes. Scarr's gaze returned to the blackened body and he realized he was being drawn slowly towards it.

'God, help me, please help me to stop – I don't want this. I don't –'

Somehow, he lost his balance and found himself falling straight into what remained of the stinking corpse whose near-fleshless arms seemed to reach up and clasp him in an unbreak-able embrace. Scarr screamed and screamed and screamed.

Chapter 13

FALLING OFF HIS NARROW sofa, Scarr found himself still screaming. 'No! No,' he shouted as he started awake on hitting the floor, sweating heavily and breathing like a wind-broken horse. Gradually he got control of his thrashing heart and finally managed to bring his breathing back to something resembling normal. What happened to him? What a nightmare he was having. Where did he go? Who did he see? All he seemed to remember was seeing an age-blackened corpse, but didn't know whose it was. Yet somehow, the feeling surrounding it all scared the hell out of him, with a creepy sense that bony hands were grasping for him, trying to pull him back. Cautiously and slowly he let his eyes check about the room, fearing that odious body might yet be present. Certainly its atmosphere was. Who was it who died in such wretched circumstances? The question without an answer worried him. Climbing up off the floor, he noticed there was something different about himself, but couldn't quite get what it was. Then he had it. The head cold! It was completely gone and this made him feel like a new man. Yes, that's what it was. He was ready to face the day. Pale sunlight was streaming through the windows, which he had a vague recollection of being blacked out. This was nonsense, he never blacked out the windows, not even to run sensitive information on the computer. Now in this light he hadn't immediately noticed that his computer was switched on. He ran across to it and saw Bob Carter's details on the screen. Then he remembered what this day was: Christmas Day, and its significance. Today he was going to bust Mr Robert Carter and put him where he belonged, only now strangely, he felt little inclination to do so. Why was that?

Stepping over to the front door, Scarr was surprised to find it unlocked. Well, what did it matter, he wasn't robbed in the night. On the walkway as he looked out his neighbour was emerging from her door. He greeted her warmly, wishing her a merry Christmas. At this she turned immediately and smiled, then hurried back inside as if in shock at seeing him. Puzzled at her behaviour, he went to the walkway windows and looked down on to the open area between the apartment blocks. Kids on new bicycles were struggling to ride them on the snow, while others on snowboards were zooming down the slippery ramps, having a great time. Scarr checked the time and ran back into his apartment and found his phone and punched Belle's number on speed-dial. It went straight to her message minder.

'Belle, it's me, I overslept – this morning of all mornings. Call me when you pick this up.' He clicked off the phone and ran through to the bathroom to shower and shave; then he put on a clean shirt and a tie, along with his suit, wanting to be particularly presentable today. What he felt then were pangs of hunger, like he hadn't eaten for a week. In the fridge all he found was a few dried-up slices of coconut cheese and a shrivelled onion. There wasn't even a piece of bread and certainly nothing to put on it anyway. The sort of life he must have been leading was a complete puzzle to him. But there was something more important he had to do rather than hunt around for breakfast.

With no time to delay, Scarr dived out of his apartment,

pulling the front door shut. He turned with his bunch of keys, but eschewed all the locks. Flying around the stairs landing, he bumped into Mrs Turner, who dropped her meagre shopping, dinner-for-one, which Scarr reached out and caught before it hit the deck.

'Merry Christmas, Mrs Turner,' he said again, giving her back her dinner along with a warm smile. Being over her shock at her new neighbour, she responded with a smile as he plunged on down the stairs.

The ground was slippery with the white stuff as Scarr tried to hurry across the open area while kids ran along the paths with their new gear, having no problem with balance. He grabbed one as he came towards him on his snowboard. It was the tall teenager who had been hassling his neighbour. As he gave him a frank look, he noticed how good-looking he was and thought about how many hearts he might break.

'What?' Elroy said, defensively, ready to flee, but didn't. 'It wasn't me. It wasn't,' he insisted.

'Of course it wasn't,' Scarr said sincerely, which momentarily threw the tall lad. 'What?' He laughed and shook his head. 'It was you, wasn't it?'

'What?' Elroy wanted to know, and then began to relax, like he knew this was a game rather than any kind of nicking, especially when he saw the banknotes Scarr pulled from his trouser pocket.

'Is the Indian corner shop open today?'

'Are you kidding, man? On Christmas day?'

Mistaking what was being said to him, Scarr said, 'Well, where is there a shop that's open, Elroy?'

'Are you kidding, man,' Elroy repeated in the exact same tone. 'Rama ain't a Christian man. Anyway, he never closes.'

'Does he have any flowers, do you think?' he asked, proffering the two twenty-pound notes. 'Could you buy some for me and deliver them to the address I'm going to give you? And a box of plain chocolates. Would you?'

Elroy considered the money in Scarr's hand with suspicion, as if believing it might be a trick, then watched him scribble an address. 'How d'you know I won't just take the money and split, man?'

Scarr smiled at the response. 'Only a thief would do such a thing, Elroy. And I know you're a straight-shooter who I can trust.'

A surprised Elroy stood a little straighter at that point, then plucked the banknotes from Scarr's hand. 'How much do I spend on flowers?'

'You can decide that.'

'Then what do I do with them?'

'Take the flowers here.' He gave the young man the piece of paper with the address on it. 'The chocolates go up there –' pointing to his landing. 'You know, that nice old lady, Mrs Turner. You might want to say hello to her. She'd probably welcome a friendly face, especially today.'

Slightly confused, Elroy started away, then turned back. 'You really trust me, man? Right.'

'Exactly right, Elroy.'

That sent him bounding away, a changed young man.

Aware of eyes on him, Scarr turned and sees the dog staring at him. 'You again. Have you got any new tricks today?'

The dog remained unmoving. 'Thought not. C'mon.' The dog came running to him and they started across the open compound together. As they walked on the slippery snow, the four legs steadier than the two, a snowball whacked into the back of Scarr's head. Turning, he saw the Space Invader Kid from the market, who froze, uncertain, until he saw Scarr scoop up a handful of snow, then he said, 'Merry Christmas,' and ran away, laughing.

In her depressing little office, made more depressing on this particular day, Belle was banging about in a foul mood, opening file drawers, pulling out forms and slamming shut the drawers again with no apparent purpose; she then went across to her computer to check for emails when she heard Scarr come in, but was in no frame of mind to be civil to him.

'I have people who care about Christmas,' she barked without looking up at him, 'even if you don't, Eddie.'

'Yes, I'm sorry, Belle. Sorry I'm late. I had a really disturbing night.'

This caused Belle to stop abruptly and look round at the man, and his dog, unable to keep surprise off her face. 'What?' she said with open-mouthed astonishment, then noticed how he was dressed. 'Is that . . . ? Did you actually say sorry? Where did you learn that word? Well, I suppose it is Christmas and you pulled it from a cracker. And the suit, Eddie?'

'I've changed my mind about going after Bob Carter. I want to hit that wretch Guli instead – make his life a complete misery.'

Belle found herself breathing quickly and if she wasn't

already sitting down, she certainly would have had to sit. Finally recovering herself, she said, 'What makes you think Aram Guli's around?' She knew Scarr had amazing abilities at ferreting out information, only he wasn't listening.

'Is anyone else coming in – I understand if they don't want to.' He picked up the kettle from the kitchen area – not a real kitchen, just a kettle, some cups, a hot-plate and sink – checked there was water in it and plugged it in, but didn't switch it on.

'Detective Inspector Clarence is standing by if we need him. If you insist on going ahead with this, it's basically you and me.'

With a shake of the head, Scarr said, 'You go home, Belle. Go home to mum and Teddy. I'll do this.'

'On your own? Don't be stupid –' Again, that brought her up short, now believing there was something wrong with Scarr. 'Teddy? You actually remembered my daughter's name?' Scarr turned back to switch on the kettle, then gave her a sheepish look. 'Are you sure you're feeling all right? You had a bad cold – you haven't got a fever or worse?' She put her hand on his forehead and the feelings of concern she once had for him began to resurface. His head was quite cool. Puzzled, she asked, 'Why did you change your mind about Bob Carter?'

A deep sigh issued from Scarr and he shook his head again, and turned away to the kettle to busy himself with making some instant coffee. He was having difficulty answering her. Finally he nodded, as much in answer to himself as Belle. 'I know who was responsible for Jake's death. Only we haven't got any witnesses.' He closed his eyes, struggling with both the increasingly affecting loss of his friend and getting to what he knew he needed to face.

Belle waited, too. She was in no hurry now.

Hesitantly Scarr said, 'I shouldn't have pushed for that raid on Guli's place as I did. I didn't really care about him, I just wanted to nail Bob there . . . It's been hard to live with that, Belle, even harder to face the truth.'

'It can only get easier now,' Belle said quietly.

An unfamiliar feeling swept over him which he knew was regret when he heard Belle say what she did. He knew why, but couldn't answer her immediately.

'I always hated Christmas with no one . . . ' he said after a long silence without being able to complete the statement. 'I always seemed to be the one on the windy side of the window.'

'Eddie . . . ?' like she didn't know what to say.

Finally he got the words out that had been stuck in his throat for so long, a lifetime it seemed. 'I should never have let you go, Belle. It was so stupid. The worst day's work in my life.'

Still Belle was lost for a response and thought about feeling his forehead again in case he really was sickening; then she noticed the dog again. 'Where did the dog come from? I never knew you had a dog.'

Now focusing his attention on the dog made this situation easier for him. 'I had one as a kid – a bit like him. This one just seemed to latch on to me for some reason – no sense, of course. Look, he does tricks – I'm sure he does.' He looked into the dog's eyes and told him to beg. The dog remained unmoving, staring back at Scarr. 'Oh, you don't want to play? I see. Okay, I'll let you off as it's Christmas.'

'Are you sure you're all right, Eddie? You somehow look

different . . . Not just the suit and tie. Somehow you have a different atmosphere about you.'

'Yeah, well, I just came down from the moon on my sleigh,' he said flippantly, feeling slightly embarrassed. His eyes met hers. Both of them seemed on the brink of something, neither quite knowing what it was. 'Belle . . . ' He began and stopped.

'Yes . . . ' she said expectantly.

He faltered under her gaze. 'I'm . . . I . . . I'm sorry I got you here and spoilt your Christmas day.'

'God, you must have something seriously wrong with you. That's twice you've apologized, Eddie.'

That response disappointed him, her not seeming to accept the possibility of him being able to change. 'Get going,' he said brusquely to try to cover the confusion he was now feeling. 'Mum and Teddy will be waiting for you. You were never much good on raids anyway.'

That hurt look he'd seen on Belle's face so many times was back there now. He wanted to recall his words, but didn't know how. Why did she wait? What for, instead of just fleeing? He hoped she wouldn't resort to tears. To his relief she at last turned away, but then turned back and plunged in with, 'Look, this is silly you going on this alone. Come home with me. Spend Christmas with us – you can bring your dog, too.'

'No,' he responded in the same tone. 'I've got a couple of errands to run. You just go.'

Belle closed her eyes as if to shut out the familiar rejection as Scarr went to the computer with his coffee without looking in her direction again. She went quickly and Scarr thought he heard a sob and turned just as the door banged. What the hell was wrong with him, he wanted to know? The only conclusion he could come to was that he was a complete and utter fool.

Trying to shut out his thoughts didn't work as he brought his coffee up to his mouth and stared into the steaming black liquid without drinking it. He set the coffee down and tapped on to the keyboard. Without realising it he had called up Bob Carter's details and saw his last known address. This he sat staring at undecided before finally writing it down; then he pulled out his phone and punched up a number.

When it was answered, he said in an uncertain fashion, 'Inspector Clarence? It's Eddie Scarr. You ready?' As he listened, he turned and switched off the computer, making Bob Carter disappear. 'Sorry to spoil your day, Eric. But let's do it, shall we? Spoil someone else's.' He stood up and collected the baseball bat he kept in the office for such raids.

Chapter 14

LEADING THE WAY, SCARR crept up the threadbare carpeted stairs and stopped on the landing where he glanced at the tall, lugubrious detective with him, in his heavy Crombie overcoat that was being squeezed tight by his Kevlar vest fastened over the top of it. This man, who was stooped like he was permanently dodging a bullet and sported the thin moustache more familiar to '40s movie stars, indicated he was ready for action and motioned to his men and women who were as equally quiet on the stairs. Scarr listened at the door. After a moment Scarr gave the signal and together he and Inspector Clarence kicked in the flimsy door and led the charge, startling the trafficking soldiers and illegals gathered there. Fanning out, the detectives laid hands on them, while Scarr ran through and kicked open the office door to find Aram Guli struggling on his knees with his hand under a floorboard, trying to retrieve something from its hiding place. Scarr ran at him and jumped on the board trapping the man's fat wrist, causing him to cry out in pain.

'You want to try for your knife, Mr Guli – like you used on Jake?'

As if accepting his invitation, Guli reached into his pocket with his free hand for his switch knife when Scarr took pleasure in hitting him with the baseball bat, then again for good measure. Detectives filled the doorway, smiling, like they believed this was something worth giving up Christmas Day for.

Kim opened the door to her youngest daughter, who had been

out playing in the snow. Glancing beyond her to the street, she saw a car pull into the kerb when alarm seized her. She quickly dragged her daughter inside and slammed the door, at once calling to her husband. Her cry caused Bob Carter to spring up from the sitting room floor where he was playing with Tim as Kim hurried in and over to the window to peer out through the net curtains. Martha, Dan and Ella joined them too and peered out with anxious expressions.

'He appears to be on his own,' Kim said, as Scarr remained motionless in the car, simply leaning on the steering wheel staring through the windscreen.

'The others won't be far away, you can be sure.'

'Do you think he's waiting, giving you a chance to run, Bob?'

Shaking his head, Bob turned and picked up Tim, who had joined them at the window. He held him close and said, 'I'm not running any more. I'm spending Christmas where I belong.'

'Bob, you'll be spending it in gaol if you don't leave.'

In response Bob Carter drew his other children close to himself, trying to dispel their anxiety.

In the car Scarr continued his pensive staring out at the snow before finally turning towards the house, his mind made up. He noticed the curtains move as someone pulled back instinctively from the window. No. Having second thoughts about this, he started the car and slapped it in gear, but let the engine idle with his foot on the clutch. Yes, do it, he told himself and shut the motor off determinedly and climbed out. As he turned to reach back into the car, he saw his trusted baseball bat on the passenger seat, but reached past it to collect a couple of carrier bags. He started along the path with them, feeling a slight sense of trepidation, even apprehension as he rang the doorbell.

Almost immediately the door was thrown open by Bob Carter and the two men stood for a moment looking at each other, each unsure what the next move was. Kim and the children waited back along the hallway, their anxiety not leaving them.

'Are you going to invite me in?' Scarr asked at last in as pleasant a tone as he could muster.

'I expect your warrant gives you that right – where's your backup?'

At this point Tim ran along the hallway and hurled himself at Scarr as he stepped over the threshold, setting down the two bags. 'You can't take daddy,' the little one said, 'you can't.'

Scooping him up like a featherweight, Scarr smiled and said, 'Hang on to that fighting spirit, Tim. One day you'll make mum and dad very proud.'

Taking his youngest from Scarr, Bob said fiercely, 'We're already very proud of him.'

'I can see.' Scarr gave him a frank look. 'It's over, Bob –'

Misunderstanding, Bob Carter replied, 'I'm not going anywhere, not today.' And his wife, not hearing any of the exchange clearly, flew along the hall, followed by the other children, 'You could at least let him have Christmas with us –'

'What about all the other Christmases?' Scarr asked her.

Anxiety still blocking her reading of this situation, Kim continued, 'This might be Tim's only – you –' She couldn't get to it and Bob held her back from physically attacking Scarr.

'It won't be, Kim,' Scarr told her, 'I promise – you need

to take him back to see that gardener in the walled garden –' Where the hell that came from Scarr didn't know and was as confused about it as the Carters appeared. 'I've called off the dogs – the dog. Me. I'm sorry I made your life such a misery.'

'What's this, Scarr? Now you're coming here to mock us?'

'I wish I had developed that sort of humour, Bob.' He turned to leave, but Bob Carter stepped out and stopped him. 'What's happened? Did Jake's killer suddenly confess?'

Scarr sighed apologetically, without meeting his eyes. 'Sort of – we collared Aram Guli this morning. He suspected you were working undercover, so he was feeding us false information to implicate you.' He sighed again, then turned on the doorstep and looked beyond Bob at Kim and the children. 'Merry Christmas!' he said without irony, then nodded and departed quickly, leaving the stunned Carters staring after him as he climbed into his car and drove off.

Martha spotted the carrier bags in the hall. 'He's left his bags.'

Already Tim was pulling out crackers, toys, satsumas and a jar of pitted cherries. 'Pit-ted cherries – what is pit-ted cherries?' he wanted to know, looking up at his dad.

'Cherries you can't choke on, you twat!' Ella told him.

Having driven around undecided for an hour or more, Scarr made his next house call with even greater trepidation, to Belle's address. There was no telling what the reception would be, but he wanted more than anything to be part of Belle's family, even though he knew her mother didn't much care for him. He hoped it wasn't her who opened the door.

Bad luck, Scarr! It was Angela who opened the door, wiping her hands on a kitchen towel. She stepped back in surprise. 'My God!' she said. Fortunately the apartment door opened on to the main sitting room, where Belle was sitting on the floor playing a game with Teddy. Scarr remained at the door with a carrier bag and the dog. 'Man and dog. Well, at least the dog's welcome.'

Belle rose from the floor with an admonishing, 'Mum!' Then to Scarr she said, 'Inspector Clarence called me. Result.'

Not wanting this to be about work, Scarr said, 'Did you get the flowers?'

'Where did you find them?' Angela said pointedly. 'In the rubbish bin? They were half-dead.'

'Mum! – I can speak for myself, you know –'

'They were all I could get.'

An awkward silence fell between them, when Angela simply rolled her eyes and went back to the kitchen, throwing over her shoulder, 'Men, you're better off without them.'

'What's she, the help? Maybe you should sack her.' Belle laughed louder than the joke was worth, then covered her mouth to try to stop herself. 'I shouldn't have come really –'

'I can invite someone to my own home – even a man. Come in.' There was another awkward moment before Scarr stepped inside the warm apartment. There seemed to be many awkward moments for Scarr now. 'I'm forty-two,' Belle said quickly. 'Mum still treats me like a child.'

'Well, you are still her child.' That left yet another awkward moment. 'Look, I wasn't saying you are, you know – are you, forty-two, I mean? I didn't know. Look, I brought a few things – I didn't mean –'

'You're here, Eddie, and well. Calm down, it's all right.'

Belle opened the bag he offered and he took out a box of chocolates. 'They are vegan,' he said quickly, then noticed Teddy sitting watching this exchange. He winked at her and she turned away abruptly. 'They'll please mum.' She found a bottle of wine and stem ginger, along with a Lego set.

Scarr wasn't familiar with present-giving.

Unobtrusively as he could manage, he moved over and crouched on the floor by Teddy, who studiously ignored him. Unnoticed, the dog simply curled up in front of the gas fire like it was right at home. Persevering, despite being ignored, Scarr picked up a piece of puzzle. 'I didn't know there were puzzles at Christmas still. That's all I ever got – second-hand with bits missing. I think this piece goes –'

'Leave it,' Teddy said angrily and snatched it away from Scarr.

'Teddy, that's not very polite,' Belle said, stepping over to them. 'Eddie brought us some very nice things.'

Taking an instant dislike to him, and making an inaccurate assumption, Teddy said, 'I don't care. He's not my proper dad. I hate him. I hate him.' With that she jumped up off the floor and rushed out in tears, Belle went after her with an admonishing, 'Teddy, please.'

Glancing over at the dog, Scarr advised, 'Don't make yourself too comfortable, fella.' Now he glanced around the room and noticed how inviting it was compared to his stark dwelling. No one would die here unnoticed, he thought and at once didn't know where that thought came from. He'd be ashamed to invite anyone back to his place, much less Belle. She had such good taste. How did he ever imagine he could come back into her life and was about to slip away when Belle returned, apologising.

'She's over-excited. She was up so early. I'm sorry.'

'It's no more than I deserve, Belle.'

'My, you really have changed.'

After another one of those moments, Scarr said, 'Why didn't you tell me about Teddy?'

Now it was Belle's turn to feel awkward and answer with a half-shrug as she avoided his look.

'I should go.' He didn't want to but persuaded himself he should when Belle said nothing. 'Yes, I've got to go.'

'You don't have to,' she said at last. 'Look, Eddie, you must understand that you have to work at relationships, especially with women – of all ages! Mum's making Christmas dinner. It's vegan, but with all the trimmings.'

'I've been following your dietary regime for some time, not eating as well as you lot, I'm sure.' He hesitated. 'I've got to go. There is something I have to do, Belle.'

'Not work. Not today.'

'It's something I have to try to put right if it's not too late.' Again he hesitated, almost afraid to ask. 'Can I come back?' Now he waited almost breathlessly as Belle considered this. He added quickly, 'I really would like to work on those relationships. There's a lot to make up for, especially with Teddy and you.'

'You are a surprising man. I began to think nothing would change you.'

'I don't want to disappoint you. I'm terrified in case I do.'

'Why is that? Do you think you'll turn back into the old Eddie Scarr at midnight?'

'I'm afraid I might, Belle.'

'Well, in that case perhaps I could have something on account other than those chocolates from the nice you, should that nice you disappear.'

This puzzled Scarr. 'Like what?' he said not reading the signals as Belle leaned in and kissed him hard on the mouth. Yes, he had to understand about working on relationships.

Chapter 15

SCARR FOUND THERE HAD been no change in the circumstances for the Achebe family at the detention centre where they were housed. He wasn't sure why he had expected there to have been any. The place was overcrowded and the superintendent in charge of things was at his wits' end over where to find beds for everyone. At first, he thought Scarr was bringing him more asylum seekers to house and feed. Instead, he brought flowers, and children's toys. No one had ever turned up at their door with presents for these people.

'Mrs Achebe and her children are not flight risks,' Scarr assured him.

The superintendent looked at him with a worried expression, before noticing his clothes and then his credentials. Clearly, this visitor was official and genuine and so he began to apologize. 'We couldn't find anywhere for her to be with the children. Not at this time of year,' he explained. 'But it's a bit unusual to release them, as you suggest, without some sort of okay from the Home Office. No one there works over Christmas, nor much any other time of the year from what I can see –' He looked round sharply at Scarr as if fearing he had spoken out of turn.

A reassuring nod was how Scarr responded. He knew what duds they were at the Home Office, having had many dealings with them. Not one of those working there seemed to have a single idea about how to solve such problems. Stepping into a room that was about twenty feet by thirty, he stopped. Here were forty or more bodies sitting or lying around, looking totally dejected, each crowding the personal space of another. Certainly none imbibed with the Christmas spirit and some of them were surely Christian. Mrs Achebe and her three children were sitting on a quilt of some kind in the corner of the room. There were no other children around, a few men and the rest mostly young women.

'Can you supervize them properly here like this?' Scarr asked, putting the superintendent on the spot. 'They shouldn't be in a mixed room. Can you guarantee safeguarding? In addition, she could prove a danger to herself and her kids if you can't manage to watch her twenty-four/seven.' By this time the superintendent was looking ashen. 'No, you don't want those sorts of safeguarding problems, especially not at this time of year.'

'I'd say not, Mr Scarr.'

Scarr nodded approvingly and went along the room to collect the Achebes, feeling quite pleased that their nightmare was about to end.

The suburban street he took them to was busy with kids playing in the snow while their parents rested after a hectic few hours. From the car he watched Mrs Achebe lead her children along the path to a '50s semi-detached house situated on a busy road and ring the doorbell. They turned back to look at Scarr, not quite believing what was happening. When the door opened an equally thin Ethiopian woman shrieked with delight and disbelief at the sight of her sister with her children. Other children appeared in the doorway behind her with curious looks. Scarr smiled and put the car in gear. A good outcome, but not for the hundreds of asylum-seekers trapped in limbo.

He could only deal with one problem at a time.

Coming through the sitting room with tea things, Belle set the tray down on the table where the remnants of a feast were. Angela may not have liked him but she didn't spare him when it came to pushing food his way like she must have believed he'd not eaten in a very long while, if ever. This kind of hospitality was almost overwhelming his senses and he had no real understanding why he had for so long denied himself. Fear, he assumed, fear of being rejected again. Reminding himself he was no longer that rejected little boy on the windy side of the window and hadn't been for a long while did no good. Fear wasn't something that readily responded to reason, not when it was so deeply entrenched.

As much as he enjoyed being among these people, he didn't feel entirely accepted as part of this family, even though he had no doubt that Teddy was his daughter. Here he was sitting on the edge of an armchair, not feeling he had the right to sit back or sink deeply into it and relax as he watched Teddy kneeling at the coffee table building a robot with the Lego set he had brought. Angela was snoozing in the other armchair, having a well-earned rest, the dog lying on her feet like a comforter; Belle was pouring the fine Taiwanese Oolong tea she so liked. The happy family. Would his inclusion, if it ever happened, make them any more complete?

With a growing sense of impatience, Teddy turned from her concentrated task and said grudgingly, 'Look, if you really must help, I suppose you can.' Startled by this, Scarr's heart leapt. Was this heading towards the breakthrough he had been hoping for? Even with the caveat which swiftly followed: 'Make sure you do as I say and use the right bits.'

Kneeling on the floor besides her, Scarr said, 'You'll have to show me what to do.' Then after working for a few minutes Teddy let out a deep impatient sigh which slightly alarmed him. 'Have I missed something? Tell me what I've missed?'

'You missed my school concert,' she informed him crossly. 'I was the second angel.'

'Did anyone record it?' he asked, looking at Belle. Before she could answer Teddy jumped up and retrieved Belle's phone when, with a couple of swipes, she got the recording of the school concert and the angel chorus. Scarr took the phone to watch. He disliked watching things on the tiny screen, but here he was now mesmerized.

Leaning against him and pointing, Teddy said, 'There! That's me there. Look.'

'I am looking. I can see. You are an angel –' Sitting on his haunches, he re-ran it as Teddy went back to working on her Lego robot. His gaze fell into the middle distance and became unfocused as a great sadness overcame him. He didn't notice Belle at his side offering him tea until she said, 'Eddie.' Then he took the tea and buried his face in the cup. 'What if this is all just part of a dream I had, Belle?'

'It seems to me everything in life is either a dream or a nightmare. You have to work out which one you want to be in.'

'I've missed so much living by making people miserable. You, Teddy . . . . My sister Fran . . . .' Another of those awkward moments filled the silence again.

After waiting for him, Belle said, 'Do you know where she is?'

With a curt shake of his head – 'I haven't seen her since –' He avoided Belle's eyes, then when he dared look at her, he could see she knew he was lying. 'I arrested her once. What sort of man does that to his sister?'

'One who's scared, maybe.'

'Scared of what?' he answered, like he didn't know.

Being a straight shooter, Belle articulated it for him directly. 'Being hurt, being left again. Being vulnerable in case, like before, someone who is important to you doesn't show up.'

'You know about that, too?'

'I looked up your file. Computer records are pretty comprehensive, they don't allow any of us to hide. Do you know where she lives?'

'If she's still here – she moved around a lot.'

'It's a start, Eddie.'

He thought about that, then sighed. 'No. Let's forget it.' He closely inspected the Lego model and saw a piece that Teddy had missed. Scarr pointed it out to her.

'I know that,' Teddy said sharply and took the piece from him.

Turning back to Belle, wanting to be persuaded, Scarr said, 'I doubt she'd want to see me. Why would she, not after what I did?'

'It wasn't very charitable.'

'I'd like to meet your sister,' Teddy put in. Clearly, she had been following their conversation as she worked the Lego. 'She's my auntie and I haven't got any others.'

Scarr lowered his head, shame-faced. 'I wasn't very nice to her, Teddy.'

'Oh, but you're quite nice now and quite good at making Lego models and gran likes your dog. So do I.'

'Why don't you try, Eddie. Unless you reach out you won't ever know. Perhaps her heart is bigger than you think.'

It was all the encouragement Scarr needed.

Franny Dolittle, having been married to a Brian Dolittle – who pretty much did as little as he could when they were married – didn't bother to change her name when she divorced him. Nor did she ever look at the customers who came to George Zhong's Chinese 'medicine' parlour. They were mostly all men all wanting the same thing, only very rarely did women come through the door, then mostly to enquire prices and what was available on behalf of a man. By rote she laid out the bill of fare with the prices, but most knew what they wanted off the menu. Still she repeated what was on offer in a disinterested fashion. 'Twenty-five pounds acupuncture or herbal, massage forty pounds or sixty for the full hour of herbal.' There followed a long silence, which somehow she didn't think was indecision on the customer's part – she had a good instinct for such things, and finally steeled herself to look at the punter, instantly recognising who and what he represented. 'Don't you people ever have a day off?' she said vehemently.

Gripping the edge of the booth counter, trying to check his rising anger as he felt himself slipping back into his old mode, Scarr said, 'Don't your lot? Today of all days.'

'Are you serious? Suddenly you've got religion? Don't you

know we're like Social Services – all the support some lonely people have? At least we only take their money, we don't take their liberty like your rotten lot. Anyway, you're out of luck, pal. We're all paid up.'

'This is not an official visit, Fran.'

'Then it's eighty pounds to you, as it's Christmas.'

'No, I just want to talk.'

'Then try a therapist, why don't you? Now leave or I'll call the boss.'

As Scarr's anger, along with bitter memories, continued to rise, the wrong words bubbled forth from him and he regretted them the moment they left his mouth. 'That's your choice, just like working in this dive is, or dumping me in that care home and not coming back.'

With that Franny leaned into the microphone in the booth and barked, 'George! Trouble-maker out front –'

'No, Fran, I'm sorry, I didn't – look, I said I'm sorry.' This didn't make any difference to her agitation and she signalled the boss again via the microphone, so Scarr grabbed hold of her to stop her. 'I want you to come home with me –'

'You've got to be kidding –! Attila the Hun of Welfare? What is it you want to do,' she mocked, 'check all our insurance contributions are up to date?'

Fighting him off only made Scarr hold on to her more tightly as the triple chinned Buddha-like George Zhong ran through from the back, rapping in Chinese and seizing hold of Scarr; then recognizing him, he switched to Cockney English of a fashion.

'Oh Gawd, sorry guv – so sorry – didn't recognize you – you

look different.' Then he turned to Franny, jabbing her with his finger. 'Leave it out, Fran, this one ain't a punter –'

The vehemence that hadn't really left her reared again in Scarr's direction, 'You see how you scare people –?'

Trying to take control, Zhong said, 'I told you to bloody-well leave it out,' and reached into the booth and shoved her with his pudgy hand. That caused Scarr to shove him harder, causing him to stagger and almost fall.

'Don't you dare lay a hand on her, not ever again.'

Now Franny flew out of the booth and pulled her brother off her boss. 'Just leave him be, you bully –'

Turning in surprise – 'He doesn't push my sister around –'

'Sister -?' Zhong echoed in panic. 'She never say –'

'Please don't make things worse, Eddie. Just go.'

'Look, can we go someplace and talk? Please,' Scarr pleaded in a calm and reasonable tone. 'Please,' he said again and waited for the unyielding Franny to respond. When she didn't, he gave Zhong an apologetic shrug and left.

Across the street from the medicine parlour, Scarr stood on the pavement with his phone pressed to his ear, saying in a despondent voice, 'What do I do now, Belle? She won't talk to me.'

'It depends how much you care, Eddie. If she really matters to you, then it's worth persisting,' came the answer. Only Scarr didn't know how to progress this if his sister wouldn't talk to him. Standing staring across at her didn't seem to do it.

How long did this over-dressed loon intend to stay on the other side of the street staring like that, Franny wondered as she looked up yet again and slid her eyes in his direction? The cars going back and forth on the road frequently cut off sight of him, but he was still a distraction. Customers might start to think he was an undercover cop watching the place, which was sort of true. Reaching under the counter for a 'Back in five minutes' sign, she taped it to the window and stepped out of her booth. Nipping through the fast-moving traffic, she approached her brother. Brother? She hadn't thought of him in those terms since he sent her to prison.

'I don't suppose it would do any good calling the police to you?'

'I just want to talk. I do care about you, Fran, really.'

'I know how much!' she said bitterly. 'Your caring got me a nice stretch in Holloway Prison.'

'I didn't know,' he responded promptly and looked away with the lie, then met her cold eyes and nodded. 'Yes, I did know. Of course I did. It's on your file. I'm sorry.'

'You're sorry? Oh well, that's all right then.' Without awaiting a reply, she said, 'I had nothing when I came out. I couldn't even get benefits thanks to people like you. Look, just go away, and stay away – you scare the punters.' She started away but couldn't find a break in the traffic.

'Now I feel about as helpless as that kid who you left in care –'

'What else could I do, Eddie?' Franny said, rounding on him angrily and causing passers-by to glance in her direction and quickly avert their eyes, not wanting to be drawn into this. 'D'you think it was easy leaving you there? Seeing your little lip drop? Hearing your sobs and being afraid to look back at you? I heard your sobbing all the way down the drive. I cried myself to sleep at night hearing it; sometimes sleeping rough in a doorway something would disturb me and I'd start awake thinking it was you who had come back to me. You were all I had, my only friend. Leaving you was the last thing I wanted to do. But I couldn't help it, Social Services said that was where you had to be and I didn't know what else to do –'

This rooted Scarr to the spot; he felt deep shame as he watched Franny try to recover her emotions. He started forward with an apologetic 'Fran,' only to have her push him away with, 'Look, I said to go. Get away from me. This is my life now.'

Caring about other people was to risk suffering yourself, Scarr had recently learned and was getting some painful lessons. 'All I ever thought about was my own misery,' he said, 'about paying you back and all those who hurt me, not about how they were feeling or what they might be suffering. I've only just begun to understand how you couldn't help what you had to do, any more than some of those people I hounded for cheating the benefits system could help their circumstances, or me for mine – being left in that home.'

At this point Franny lost it and began to cry. As tears streamed down her face, Scarr hesitated to reach out to her, then when he finally did, she shrugged him off and hurried blindly across the street through horn-blaring traffic, trying to get to the safety of her booth. Unthinkingly, Scarr flew after her with the same disregard of moving vehicles when a blaring horn and screech of tyres caused Franny to turn and scream as she saw a white van plough into her brother.

Chapter 16

IN THE PRIVATE ROOM at the hospital where Scarr was put on account of him not being expected to live, his head and upper body swathed in bandage, he opened his eyes momentarily. In the hazy light he saw Jake Marlow by the bed and smiled at him, or thought he did.

'Jake! Where's the mat of files you had weighing you down?' he asked.

'What files are they, Eddie?'

'Did I make it? Is this it? The right side of the fence . . . ?'

As if out of nowhere, Rachel stepped forward and joined Jake, shaking her head. 'Unlucky, Mr Scarr.'

'I think I'm about ready to join you,' Scarr said.

'Someone's not sure about that,' Rachel said and shook her head again. 'First you've got a bit more work to do on those relationships.'

Scarr sighed a disappointed sigh. 'Oh, not that again,' he said, remembering those past and future lives. Instead, he closed his eyes and drifted off.

Pacing in the corridor, Belle was almost afraid to go back into the room and confront that doctor in case Scarr's condition had worsened. She couldn't quite face that, having so briefly unearthed what she knew to be his true character only to lose him again like this. With a deep breath to fortify herself, Belle pushed into the room where the quite old junior doctor was checking Scarr's eyes with an ophthalmoscope. The doctor's movements were slow and appeared considered, but she suspected he was just tired from overwork. At last he seemed to notice her and Belle was unable to keep anxiety out of her voice when she finally found the courage to ask, 'How is he? Is he –? Will he –?' she couldn't say the words.

'Are you his wife?' he asked, like he hadn't spoken to her earlier and previously made the same enquiry.

'No, the mother of his child.'

'Oh yes,' he said vaguely. 'Well, mummy, we can't seem to wake him up, get him to regain consciousness. All very strange.'

'What do you mean, can't? What's wrong with him? Has something else happened to his brain?'

'I'm not sure we know,' the doctor said. 'All the indicators are such that he should wake up, but he doesn't. He has a strong pulse, good blood pressure, the CT scan looked okay; nothing had come adrift inside his head. It's like there's something holding him back. It's almost as if he no longer wants to be here. Do you have any idea what the reason might be?'

Belle thought about that. Was it guilt? Did he subconsciously feel he hadn't made sufficient amends? 'He's been through some big emotional upheavals.'

'Is he a fighter?' the doctor asked.

Could he fight hard enough for himself to overcome his past? Belle hoped so and nodded in response to the question.

'That might be his best chance,' the doctor told her. 'That and those who matter most to him talking to him – try to talk him out of this coma, if you will, mummy.'

After he had departed, Belle stood wondering if she had imagined the words of this strange doctor. He was like no other she had ever encountered. Sitting at the bedside, Belle took Scarr's hand and squeezed it. 'Eddie. I love you, Eddie. Don't leave me, don't leave us, not now we've found you again.'

For over an hour she sat there talking non-stop to him like this until her mother arrived with Teddy. At once his daughter sat on the bed and started stroking his face and chatting to him about the Christmas presents she had received, telling him how the Lego robot they'd made could move; then without warning she changed her tone, giving him clear and firm instructions: 'Daddy, wake up now. Yes daddy, you can wake up. You must do so right now.'

The deep coma Scarr was in seemed to remain as deep, but then after a few moments his eyelids flickered. The images he saw were still a hazy blur, but he thought he saw Bob Carter at the bed with his youngest son, who was touching his face, telling him to wake up. He felt himself on the very edge of consciousness and might have believed he was about to wake up if he hadn't seen Jake Marlow standing in the room with the young woman, Rachel. They were watching him and waiting. Why were they here? Yes, they were waiting for him to join them.

'Eddie, darling. Wake up. Please.'

'Daddy you can wake up, you can,' Teddy was saying to him. And looked round to the door with her mother as Franny entered the room. After a moment's hesitation she came over the bed.

'Eddie, Franny's come to see you. She's here, Eddie. We all love you very much, Eddie. You won't be left ever again.'

'I'm sorry, Eddie, I should have tried harder instead of

giving up after they turned me away from that care home. I'm
so sorry I left you in that awful place.' The only response from
her brother were his eyes falling shut again and Franny seemed
disappointed and downcast.

'I think deep down he knows how hard you tried, Fran,'
Belle said, putting a comforting arm around her, while seeking
as much support as she was giving.

Through his clouded vision, Scarr could see Jake now standing close by his bed. 'You don't want to come this way with us,'
he was saying, 'not yet.'

'I don't?'

Jake laughed. 'There's no one to nick here. They're all up
to date. Anyway, a lot of people are praying for you. Look at
this.' He took him on a trip to the house of Mrs Achebe's sister
where the whole extended family were praying in a language he
didn't understand, all he understood was his name, Mr Scarr,
as it was said over and over. Then Jake took him to the Carters'
home where Tim was leading them in prayer. Next, they were
in a church where Mrs Turner was praying with Elroy and a
bunch of other kids.

'Thanks, Jake,' Scarr said in a clear voice that caused Belle
to look up startled, with the equally startled Franny and Angela. Teddy simply smiled and clapped loudly like this was what
she was expecting to happen finally.

Epilogue

EXHAUSTED, BUT LOOKING VERY pleased, Belle sat in bed with her new baby. Despite all the warnings about being an 'older mum' and possibly having trouble birthing, she had, with Eddie's encouragement, resisted this being turned into a full medical procedure. Seven years and eight months ago she had been anxious at the birth of Teddy and allowed the medics to take over, but then didn't have Eddie with her; here Eddie was at her side all the way, with Teddy and Angela, and Franny, not very far away, and she had needed very little help from anyone. The whole while the dog was sitting patiently at the hospital entrance waiting for Scarr to reappear and tell him everything was fine. All present were eager to have a cuddle with the wee one, including the dog probably, but Belle was reluctant to give up her new baby. Finally, she relented and handed over Marigold – which Teddy decided she should be called – first to Scarr, who looked more pleased than someone winning the lottery. For him this was a big lottery win.

'She has your eyes, Belle and my chin, and your pretty mouth Teddy,' Scarr said. 'Let's hope she has your sweet disposition, Angela.' He winked at her as he handed his new daughter to his older daughter, who was pressing forward wanting to hold her. Angela pressed in too and put her hand on Teddy's back to steady her like she imagined her granddaughter might stumble with baby. Scarr sat on the edge of the bed and took Belle's hand. 'How am I ever going to win an argument around five females?' he said.

'That's easy, dad,' Teddy said, glancing round at him, 'don't argue. Just do as we say and it'll be fine.'

Now the dog appeared at the ground-floor window and barked, getting everyone's attention, then it put its nose against the glass making them laugh. Scarr glanced at his mother-in-law, then Franny, neither of whom made any move as they waited to hold Marigold, so he got up and eased open the window so as not to exclude the dog. Straightaway it jumped into the room.

'You want to hold Baby Marigold as well?' he asked. The dog responded immediately by sitting down and putting its front paws up in a begging position. Scarr laughed. The dog could do tricks after all.